Saints &
Sinners

LOUISE TURNER &
WANDA JENNINGS

BOOK TWO OF THE MAGNOLIA
MANOR SERIES

Printed in the United States of America
First Printed May 2020
Cover Art by Victoria L. Hawkins
Publisher: Southern Willow Publishing, LLC
ISBN: 978-1-7347354-0-6

"Friendship is certainly the finest balm for the pangs of disappointed love."
—Jane Austen,
Northanger Abbey

There is nothing more powerful than a strong tried and true friendship. Friendships come in many forms and can span generations. It is to all friendships, far and wide, that we dedicate this book.

❧Chapter One❧

"Ruby, I've got something I need to say," Jameson said suddenly.

Ruby's eyes lit up as she turned towards him on the bed. This was it. Jameson was finally going to ask her to marry him. They had been talking about it for so long and now was just as good a time as any. They had been dating for six years and Ruby just graduated with a teaching degree from Rhinestone Community College. His bedroom wasn't the most romantic of places, but Ruby didn't mind.

"I think we need to take a break," Jameson whispered.

Ruby looked at him in shock, her face now a ghost white pallor. "What did you say?" she cautiously asked.

"I think we need to take a break, but just for this summer," he replied. His voice had dropped to a low whisper and his hands were shaking. "I don't want to, but I think it's for the best. Between interning at Hastings & Barnes and the bar exam in September, I just can't keep up. You know how my folks are. I've got to keep my nose to the grindstone. It's not fair to drag you down this road I'm barely keeping up with myself. Just enough time for me to get my head on straight and figure out what I'm supposed to be doing with my life, ok?"

Jameson studied Ruby's face as she mulled over his rambling. She wasn't crying, but he could see the storm brewing. Ruby didn't show emotions like most of the other girls he knew. He had always admired her for that. She didn't explode in anger or cry at the drop of a hat. She was strong and wasn't as fragile as stereotypical women were. He knew she was looking forward to spending time together this summer now that he had graduated law school. The driving over an hour back and forth between Rhinestone and Junction wasn't the worst of commutes, but it got tiring over the years. He had been looking forward to it, too, but he was exhausted and could hardly keep up with all the responsibilities on his shoulders.

"I don't understand, Jameson. I thought you wanted to ask me to marry you, but here you are saying you want us to break up," Ruby whispered. Her lip trembled and she sighed heavily. "Your parents probably think it's a good idea, right?"

"Don't be like that, please. They love you Ruby. They just think we're moving too fast is all," Jameson explained. "They just don't want us to rush into things and, you know, we need to have a good foundation."

"We've been together since I was sixteen, Jameson. I'm twenty-two now. That's six years," Ruby replied. "Are you saying all that has been a waste of time? If you didn't want to get married, why keep this charade up?"

"I do want to get married! And it's not a break up, it's a pause. Yea, a pause. We have the whole summer to think about things and timelines and all that. Maybe the summer is just a pause button for both of us," he explained.

"I don't need a pause. I thought we had things pretty well planned out, but I guess I was wrong," she sighed.

"You said you weren't sure if you were going to accept that position over at the elementary school or not. And I just meant that I've gotta throw myself even deeper into studying for the bar. My daddy'll kill me if I don't pass it the first time. That's all he ever talks about, you know that. Just this summer, baby. We'll both be around town and it's not like we have to avoid each other or stop talking. We can just take this time and try to figure out our next steps. We can meet back up and figure out our lives and see where we both are in a month or so," he replied.

It wasn't that he didn't love Ruby, because he loved her more than anything. It was just that he was at a crossroads in life and if he was being honest with himself, he was drowning. He thought he was finally in the home stretch of things now that he had graduated from law school. He had thought they would have the whole summer to relax and make up for lost time. He'd planned a fishing getaway with his friends, as well as spending every other waking moment with Ruby, but Hastings & Barnes had him filing paperwork, researching for hours on end, collecting depositions, and memorizing coffee orders day in and day out. By the time he got home at night, he stayed up for hours studying under the watchful eye of James Bertram Montgomery, his father, the longest serving district attorney Rhinestone had ever had. Jameson could not balance one more thing at the moment. Not that Ruby required balancing per se. He just knew he wasn't being fair to her or to himself at the moment. He needed to pour every ounce of his focus into his career and unfortunately he couldn't focus with Ruby on the forefront of his mind.

"Ruby?" he called to her gently.

Ruby was lost in her own head thinking about how her entire summer, and maybe her entire life, had suddenly changed in an instant. Figure out their lives? She had hers pretty well figured out already. She was planning on marrying Jameson and making a beautiful family together.

"Ruby?" he called out again.

Ruby turned back towards Jameson and shook her head. She really didn't have any words to say to him at the moment. She knew if she tried to speak, she would end up crying and making a scene. She stood up and ran her fingers through her long blond hair and slipped her shoes on. She folded his weathered letterman's jacket over the back of his desk chair and kissed him lightly on his cheek. "Goodbye Jameson," she said quickly and walked down the stairs towards the kitchen. She could hear him shuffling behind her, but she resolved herself not to turn around. She was willing herself not to cry in front of him or his mother who was stirring a large pot of something on the stove.

"Ruby, wait!" Jameson reached for her arm before she could open the front door. She shook him off and fished for her car keys inside her purse.

She left Jameson standing in his driveway watching her back out of the long drive. He had not meant to insinuate that he was finished with her for good. He just needed some room to breathe and time to get his priorities straight. He knew what was expected of him and while his future plans most definitely included Ruby, he knew his future couldn't begin just yet.

Once Ruby was safely on the road away from Jameson's house, the dam broke and tears splashed out of her eyes. She hadn't seen that conversation coming at all. Not that it was much of a conversation, more like a declaration from Jameson. One that he had expected her to take calmly and rationally. But Ruby was done being calm and rational. She was tired of being the pretty arm candy for the next attorney at law in the Montgomery line of lawyers. Maybe Jameson was right after all. Maybe Ruby needed this summer to make her own plans and clear her head. If anyone could help her do just that, it was her best friends Maude and Opal.

Maude, Opal, and Ruby called themselves the Stone Sisters after Rhinestone, their beloved hometown. Together they were the tightest group of girls anyone had ever seen. They had been best friends since elementary school. If anyone could make her feel better and snap her back to reality, it would be Maude and Opal. She was supposed to meet up with them after dinner with Jameson for a slumber party anyway, so she drove straight to Maude's house where she assumed Opal would already be spread out with bowls of popcorn and a half eaten pizza in a greasy box. If Opal could manage, maybe she would sneak over some of her father's moonshine that he kept hidden in the basement. Ruby had never tried shine before, but Maude and Opal assured her it was an acquired taste and she'd soon learn to love it. Ruby wasn't so sure.

All three members of the Stone Sisters were very different. Ruby was the more straight-laced one of the group, where Opal was wild and carefree. She was what Ruby's mother referred to as a gypsy soul. She never met a stranger. To balance them out, Maude lay somewhere in the middle. Maude was tough and angsty. If truth be told, everyone was a little intimidated by Maude when they first met her. The three of them together formed an interesting pack. They would do anything for each other.

Ruby pulled her 1957 Nash Cosmopolitan next to the rose bush and knocked quietly on the back door. She wasn't sure if anyone else was there or not, but her fears were suddenly calmed when she saw Maude peeking out of the window shade a few feet away.

"Ruby! What are you doing here so early?" she asked and flung open the door. With one look at Ruby's tear streaked face, Maude knew something wasn't right. "What's going on?"

"Where is everybody?" Ruby asked.

"My parents took Joe over to Brighton for the weekend. I told them we'd hold the fort down while they were gone," Maude laughed. "What's wrong? You don't look so well."

"I'm not," Ruby swallowed hard. "It's Jameson. We broke up."

"Opal! Hurry down here!" Maude shouted up the carpeted stairwell.

"What is the world?" Opal shouted back. She took the stairs two at a time and landed gracefully in front of Maude and Ruby. "You bellowed," she bowed and laughed.

Maude elbowed her rather hard and Opal howled. "Damn't Maude! That hurt!" Opal grimaced and rubbed her side. "What was that for?"

Ruby dropped her overnight bag at her feet and whispered, "Jameson broke up with me."

Opal suddenly realized Ruby had been crying and pushed Maude out of the way to reach Ruby. She wrapped her arms around her and led Ruby up the stairs. She shouted over her shoulder to Maude who was left standing by the back door. "Well, don't just stand there! Grab her bag Maude and come on!"

Maude huffed and threw Ruby's bag over her shoulder and followed suit. She dumped the overnight bag at the foot of the bed and joined Opal and Ruby on the floor.

"Tell us everything," Opal said.

Ruby recounted her afternoon with Jameson as best she could. "So I left. I drove off and refused to look at him. I left him in the driveway standing there scratching his head," she finished.

"That man is twenty-five years old and he still jumps when his mama says boo. I'm sorry Ruby, but it's about time he learns to stand on his own two feet," Maude said.

"That's right! Not everyone naturally has all their stuff together like we do!" Opal agreed.

Ruby sighed heavily. "I know he's under so much pressure. That's what happens when you're an only child. He's the only one to carry on the family name and he's working so hard. I just don't want him to forget about me," she said tearfully.

"Maybe it's not as bad as you think," Maude said. "It's just a break. He'll probably realize in a few days or so how stupid he's being and come banging on your door begging you to let him in," she shrugged.

"And Ruby won't be there to answer!" cheered Opal.

Maude glanced over at Opal. Now was not the time for one of her harebrained ideas.

"And where will I be?" Ruby asked confused.

"Well," Opal started.

"Oh God, here we go!" Maude rolled her eyes.

"Wait, just hear me out!" Opal said and jumped up to her feet. "Maybe this is exactly what we all need!"

"What are you talking about, looney?" Maude asked.

"Well, you and I were just saying what a shame it was that we never went on our high school graduation trip. It's been four years! If not now, then when!" Opal said.

Maude nodded reluctantly, as she always did when Opal was the voice of reason. "I mean, she does have a point," Maude said to Ruby.

"Of course I do!" Opal replied.

Ruby shook her head and tried to settle them both down. "We can't just up and leave on a vacation right now! We have jobs and boyfriends, and, well. We have jobs and a life, Opal."

"We're only young once, Ruby. Or should I call you Sister Ruby of the Virgin Mary," Opal smirked. "Come on! Live a little! Please! You wouldn't let us go four years ago after high school graduation. Let's do it now! You just wrapped up college and have all summer before your next job starts. Our parents worked so hard to get us that trip and we've all been working and saving. Let's do it! Please Ruby!"

Opal was ever the dramatist when she really wanted something, but Ruby had to admit that Opal had a point. Their parents had given them all a rather lavish graduation gift of a two week trip to Italy. Ruby hadn't wanted to leave Jameson during the summers, so she kept putting it off. Maude and Opal refused to go without her, so the trip had been postponed indefinitely. Maybe she did need a few weeks on the sandy beaches in a foreign country to clear her head.

"When would we leave? We don't know how to plan a trip across the world," exclaimed Ruby.

"Oh heavens Ruby, if we only did the things we know to do, we'd never have any fun," laughed Maude.

"Y'all leave it to me," explained Opal. "I know how to make it happen! We already have our passports, so y'all just worry about packing the right clothes."

Maude rolled her eyes, "Oh sweet baby Jesus!"

"Hush up, Maude. It'll be great!" Opal quipped.

Maude chuckled. If anyone knew how to wrangle up some trouble, it was Opal! "Well, I'm in. I'm practically wasting away here in Rhinestone," Maude said.

"So, are you in?" Opal asked Ruby.

"Beaches, fancy coffee, and a once in a lifetime trip with my two best friends?" Ruby asked. The thought of it all made her smile. Opal took that smile as a sign of victory.

"Perfect! Then it's settled," Opal winked at them. "I'll take care of everything and we'll spend two glorious weeks in Italy."

~Chapter Two~

What exactly did one pack for a summer vacation in Italy? None of the Stone Sisters had ever been out of the state before, unless you counted the overnight stay in Florida when Opal went with her boss to pick up a more vibrant shade of blue hair dye for the mayor's mother's funeral. Maude bought a couple of fashion magazines at the convenience store and they read them cover to cover over the next two weeks so they wouldn't stick out like sore thumbs.

"All I plan on doing is laying on the beach all day long," Maude smiled. "If a handsome man happens to be laying next to me, so be it."

"We ain't staying on the beach all day, Maude. There's places to shop and things to do. Like cliff diving! And the food! Don't even get me started on the food! We are going to eat all the fanciest food in the world," Opal countered.

"I ain't eating all that so called fancy stuff, Opal," Maude interjected. "You never know what's really in those foreign dishes."

"Oh hush. I speak Italian and I know all the great places to go!" Opal replied.

"How so? You don't speak Italian! And you ain't ever been to Italy so don't start with that mess!" Maude said.

"Never you mind!" Opal hissed and rolled her eyes. She ignored Maude like she usually did and continued to tick off adventures on her fingertips.

Ruby couldn't help but smile. This was the trip she needed after all. When she told her parents about it, they were thrilled and said it was about time. Honestly, it wouldn't matter where the three of them were going. If they were together, they were bound to have a good time. Trouble never seemed to linger long with so much laughter in the air.

Opal said she would have everything ready in a few weeks time. Though exactly what she was planning, Ruby and Maude weren't sure. Whenever they asked her for any details, she would tell them not to worry. "It's going to be great. You'll see!" Opal assured them.

Against their better judgment, Ruby and Maude gave Opal free reign with the plans. What could really go wrong, anyway? Their parents were funding the bulk of the trip and surely they were overseeing the arrangements. How much trouble could Opal really get into?

Maude took the opportunity to work as many hours as she could down at the Lazy Dog Drive-In in the evenings after working at Coops, her dad's mechanic shop, during the day. There was no harm in having a little extra spending money for a trip like this. She thought about cleaning out her savings account to stock up on a few nice outfits because Italian men were known for liking ladies with a sense of style. But she reminded herself that they would only be gone for two weeks and she had more extensive plans for those savings anyway.

Opal spent her days working beside Mrs. Belva Sinclair at the Comb Over, the most prestigious salon Rhinestone had to offer. Anybody who was anybody came to the Comb Over to get their hair done. Belva considered Opal to be the daughter she never had. Now that her husband was already dearly departed, Belva had promised to leave her fortune to Opal, whom she considered to be the best cosmetologist this side of the Mississippi. She slipped Opal an envelope one evening and told her to enjoy her trip.

Meanwhile, Ruby tried to keep her mind as far off of Jameson Montgomery as she could. It was almost impossible to do that in a small town. Everywhere she went, someone would ask her about him. How was he doing at the law firm? Had he taken and passed the bar yet? When were they going to get married? All those questions were enough to make her feel nauseated. The pressure of it all was still getting to her. On more than one occasion, she told her mother that she had changed her mind about the trip. Then she would speak to Maude and Opal who were able to reignite her excitement in the whole adventure. Finally, two nights before they were set to leave, her mother put her foot down after Ruby had yet again decided against going.

"Ruby Morgan, I don't want to hear another word about this. You're going on this trip and that's that. It's already paid for. The plans have been made and your friends are excited. You need to get away from here for a few weeks. It's the only way you're going to put this all behind you," her mother had said. Ruby shrugged her shoulders and continued packing. She knew her mother was right, but something was still nagging at her.

Jameson had called every night since their talk and Ruby had refused to come to the phone each time. Her mother, Barbara, said she should at least tell him that she was planning on vacationing in Italy. "You know he'll be worried sick when you're gone," her mother said. They were folding the final load of shirts to pack in Ruby's large suitcase.

"I don't think I owe him anything right now, mom. I just want to get on the plane and step off into the Italian air," she smiled.

"I'm not saying you owe him anything, baby. I just know that you'd want to know if you were in his position," Barbara replied.

Ruby knew she was right, but it hurt a little less making a clean break of things. She certainly hadn't been able to get away from him in this town. Why couldn't he find out that she had left through the grapevine as well. Maybe she'd send him a postcard while on vacation. Wouldn't that start the gossip brewing again?

"I'll think about it," she promised her mother.

She was saved from any further advice by the telephone downstairs. "Ruby, it's for you, sugar!" her dad called up.

Ruby walked down the stairs a little quicker than normal. Maude was supposed to call her about their hair appointment the next day. They were going to look amazing when they walked down the steps of the plane into an adoring crowd of Italian admirers.

"Hello," she asked lightheartedly.

"Hi, Ruby. How have you been?" Jameson asked.

"Oh, it's just you," Ruby said with more gumption than she felt. Now was not the time to let him know how much she had been missing him. Now was the time to show him that she was completely over him and not waiting by the phone every evening. She was doing just fine without him. She wasn't fine of course, but Maude and Opal insisted she take this approach. They told her that she would have to fake it till she made it.

"Were you expecting someone else?" he asked. He sounded hurt.

"Actually, yes. I was," she answered curtly.

Jameson was surprised to hear this. Ruby had never been so short with him before.

"Oh, I didn't realize..." he began.

"No. Obviously you didn't," she replied before he could finish his sentence.

Jameson cleared his throat. "Uh, anyway, I heard that you and your friends are going on a trip."

"Yes, we are. Finally. You remember Maude and Opal, I'm sure," Ruby snapped. Of course Jameson knew her two closest friends. She knew her tone wasn't kind, but she was not about to give out any pertinent information about this adventure. She could almost see him squirming at the lack of details.

"How could I forget your two closest friends? Is it that trip y'all were talking about a while back?" he asked.

"Yes, the trip we've been talking about for ages. The one I never took because I was spending time with you. Since that's no longer an issue, we're going," Ruby sassed. She couldn't believe her own nerve.

"Oh, that's great," Jameson lied. He wasn't so sure that his idea of a break meant traveling the world. "How long will you be gone?"

"Right now it's two weeks, but we might stay longer," she answered. Where did that come from? She knew good and well there were no plans to stay abroad any longer than their allotted two weeks. And yet, the idea of Jameson sweating over when she would return was the tonic she had been needing.

"Oh, well, okay. Umm. Well, when are you leaving? Maybe we could, you know, have lunch or dinner or something before you go?" he offered.

"We've got so much to do to get ready. I'm not sure how we can get it all done. Maybe we can catch up when I get back. You know, once we've both figured everything out," she said with a smile.

"Oh, yeah," he muttered.

"Anyway, Jameson. It was nice of you to call, but really I am waiting to hear from someone else. We'll talk soon, okay?" Ruby said. She didn't even wait to hear his reply before she hung up the phone.

No sooner had the handset touched the receiver did it ring again. Ruby answered it without even thinking.

"Now, Jameson, really. I did tell you I was waiting on another call and," Ruby began.

"Jameson? I've never been mistaken for a man before. Weird," Maude replied.

"Oh geez! Sorry Maude! You're never gonna believe it!" Ruby laughed. She leaned back on the sofa and recounted the entire conversation she'd had moments earlier.

"How'd he know we were going on a trip?" Maude asked.

"I didn't ask," Ruby shrugged. "I turned down his lunch invitation, too."

"Serves him right! Who does he think he is wanting to go out to lunch with you? Oh my God Ruby! He thinks you're going to find a fellow over there!" Maude said wisely.

"Maybe I will," Ruby laughed.

"Maybe I will, too!" Maude laughed. "Wouldn't that be a hoot? Let's all fall in love with some Italian stud. What if we each brought an Italian home with us? Can you imagine the gossip at the Comb Over?"

"Opal's the only one crazy enough to do that," Ruby laughed. Ruby wasn't altogether sure she wanted to find another man, but it felt good to laugh.

"True," Maude agreed. "Of course, knowing Opal, she's libel to come home with a gondola!"

They burst out in fits of laughter. Their conversation soon turned to the last day of preparations for the great adventure. They decided on a time to meet and went over what items they were bringing one more time.

"And Opal still hasn't told you many of the details?" Ruby asked Maude for the millionth time.

"No. She's being very tightlipped about it all. She's really excited about it. Said she got a great deal on airline tickets. Scares me a little bit, you know. I don't really put anything past Opal. No telling what will happen. We can ask her again tomorrow while she does our hair," Maude said.

"All we have to do is get to Italy. We can sort everything else out once we get there," Ruby assured her.

They spoke for a few more minutes before hanging up. With a new bounce in her step, Ruby bounded up the stairs to her room to finish packing. This trip was going to be amazing. But honestly, her new good mood had as much to do with her conversation with Jameson as it did with the prospect of traveling the world. So he had heard about her trip and he was suddenly anxious to meet? Funny. Maybe two weeks in Italy was exactly what he needed to think about. She put the last of her things in the large suitcase and snapped the lid closed. She couldn't think of anything else she should need over there.

Maude was right. Opal was as giddy as a school girl. The next day at the Comb Over, while she brushed Ruby's long hair, Opal recounted how she had made all the reservations and credited her knowledge of the Italian language that really came in handy when she was calling overseas to speak to the hotel. Ruby looked at her in amazement. She'd known Opal all her life. Where in the world did she learn to speak Italian?

"I can tell you because you're not all uppity like Maude is sometimes. I've got us this great little place right on the beach. Only a few dollars a night. Can you believe it?" Opal bragged. She looked over at the big hair dryer to make sure Maude couldn't hear what she was saying.

"What time is the flight leaving?" Ruby asked.

"Eleven thirty. I got us a great deal. We saved so much on the tickets that we may be able to stay an extra few days," Opal was ecstatic. "Just wait till you see the hotel we're staying at. It's right on the ocean. Has the perfect view and everything!"

Ruby wasn't sure about actually staying over there any longer than the original two weeks, but she allowed herself to be swept away in her friends' good spirits. No doubt about it, this trip was exactly what the doctor ordered for all three of them.

‍Chapter Three‍

"OPAL! OPAL! Are you ready?" Maude yelled as she banged on the kitchen door of Opal's house.

"Why isn't she answering the door?" Ruby asked. She had been waiting in the car, but seeing the increasingly frantic look on Maude's face made her get out to investigate.

"I don't know. Why does Opal do or not do anything?" Maude shouted.

"She told me yesterday that everyone would all be gone to work by the time we got here to pick her up. She sounded like she was going to get up early with them so she'd be ready. Maybe she's in the bathroom. Knock a little harder," Ruby told her.

"If I knock any harder, I'll bust the door down," Maude huffed.

Ruby peered in the window at the quiet house inside. There was no movement and nothing to indicate that anyone was alive within its midst.

"OPAL!" Maude yelled again. "OPAL!"

"Wait a minute, I think I see something," Ruby said, nudging Maude on the arm.

Maude joined her at the window and they both watched in stunned horror as a pajama clad Opal came tumbling down the stairs. Opal looked around and stifled a yawn.

"Opal! I'm going to kill you!" Maude yelled loudly through the window.

Opal looked up at her friends and waved. She opened the door and let them both in. "Good morning," she said, yawning once more.

"What in the world, Opal? Are you just waking up? Please tell me you're kidding!" Maude asked.

"Yeah, what time is it?" Opal asked.

"It's time for us to go. We should have left fifteen minutes ago," Ruby informed her.

"What time is it?" Opal asked again.

"It's past eight o'clock. The time we said we would be leaving for the airport," Maude said in a huff. "Where are your bags?"

"Upstairs. I've got my beach bag ready and I've almost finished packing my clothes," Opal said proudly.

"Almost finished packing?" Maude yelled. "What do you mean you've almost finished packing?"

"Exactly what I said. I've only got a few more things to put in there. Well, maybe more than a few, but it won't take long," Opal said as she reached in the refrigerator for some milk.

"Dear God, Opal! We don't have time for you to dawdle. We've got to go," Ruby said, taking the milk that Opal had set on the counter. She smelled it and turned up her nose at the smell of spoiled milk. Ruby poured the milk down the sink and yelled up the stairs to Maude that they were coming up.

Opal, who had turned to take a glass from the cabinet, looked around for the missing glass jug of milk.

"Hey! I'm thirsty!" Opal cried.

Ruby grabbed Opal's arm and began dragging her up the stairs. "Come on! We gotta get going."

"But, I was going to get something to drink," Opal protested.

"No time for that now. We should already be on the road," Ruby said.

"Okay, okay. Hold your horses. We got time," Opal said, twisting out of her grip.

"We don't have time. We should have left twenty minutes ago. Maude you start packing. I'm going to help sleeping beauty here get ready," Ruby said, taking charge of the situation.

"I'm on it," Maude already had Opal's suitcase spread open on the unmade bed. To say Opal was almost packed was a bit optimistic. Opal had packed exactly three pairs of socks, a skimpy sundress, and a feather boa. Things were dire and there was no time to be choosy. Maude went over to Opal's dresser and began scooping up clothes with reckless abandon. Once one drawer was cleaned out, she moved to the next one. Fashion was not a priority at the moment. Making sure all of Opal's parts were covered during this expedition was the only thing that concerned Maude.

While Maude was emptying out Opal's dresser, Ruby was busy making Opal presentable for the immediate future. She threw a button down shirt at her friend which landed on Opal's head.

"Hey!" Opal shouted.

"No time!" Ruby said as she threw a pair of wadded up jeans over her shoulder. "Here, put these on!"

Opal stretched again and moseyed into the bathroom with the proffered clothes.

"And hurry up," Ruby called after her.

Maude turned to Ruby. "Hand me some of those clothes hanging up."

"Which ones?" Ruby asked.

"Whichever ones you like. I think I've got the main things covered. Just give me something that looks good," Maude suggested.

Ruby rolled her eyes looking at Opal's closet. No one had ever accused Opal of having good fashion sense.

"Have you brushed your teeth yet?" Ruby yelled into the bathroom.

"I'm getting there! Hold your horses," Opal sighed.

"Maude, we are never going to get there on time," Ruby whispered.

"Oh yes we are! Opal! Hurry the hell up! We ain't got all day!" Maude yelled.

"I'm coming!" Opal snapped.

When Opal emerged from the bathroom, she found her friends sitting on the oversized suitcase trying to force it closed.

"Can you close that one closest to you?" Maude asked, reaching between her legs trying to fasten the clasp by her right hand.

"Almost," Ruby grunted. This was not going to be an easy feat.

"Oh, you packed already? What all did you put in there?" Opal asked. For a moment it looked as though she was going to try to add things to it.

"We put your whole damn wardrobe in here. Now get your shoes on!" Maude demanded.

Ruby looked at her watch and bit her lip. "We're never gonna make it."

"Yes we will. Don't worry. I'll get us there on time," Maude said. She looked at the suitcase with a bit of concern. There was no way those clasps were going to hold. She went to the closet and grabbed a belt and laced it through the handle. "There! That should hold it. Let's go Opal!" Maude said hoisting up the suitcase with a bit of effort. Maybe they packed too much inside. There was no time to sort through it now. She pulled it to the stairs and heaved it down.

"Are we ready now?" Maude asked. Opal shrugged and Maude took that as a sign. With a quick slap on the back, Opal was soon at the bottom of the stairs with her suitcase. Maude followed two steps at a time.

"Opal, get up. We don't have all day for you to be laying around," Maude told her.

"Don't forget my pillow!" Opal hollered up the stairs. Ruby appeared behind her, pillow in hand, and grabbed Opal by the arm and pulled her out the door. Minutes later, Maude loaded Opal's suitcase into the already crowded trunk. She climbed in behind the steering wheel and waited for the other two to get in the car.

"Come on!" she shouted.

Ruby and Opal stared at each other, neither one wanting to climb into the back seat with the luggage. "Ugh, fine. I'll sit back here, but I'm getting the window seat on the plane," Ruby announced. She crawled into the back seat wedged between suitcases and pillows.

"Oh, well, if you're sure," Opal smiled. She pushed the seat back into position and hopped into the front passenger seat. She pulled a book out of her oversized beach bag and stretched her legs onto the dash. "Ahh, vacation! Italy, here we come!" Opal shouted. "Italy or bust!"

Maude peeled out of the driveway causing Ruby to almost lose her breakfast.

"Here we go!" Opal squealed.

"Maude! Slow down! I can hardly breathe back here!" Ruby yelled.

"We're on a tight schedule!" Maude replied through gritted teeth.

"What time is the flight? Twelve thirty, right?" Ruby asked.

"Nope. Eleven thirty. We're fine," Opal smiled. She stretched her arms wide and almost knocked Maude's glasses off her face.

"Um, our time or their time?" Ruby asked in a panic.

"What do you mean their time or our time? Time is time, Ruby!" Opal rolled her eyes at her friend in the back seat.

"Hartsfield Airport is in Atlanta. That's Georgia time, you dingbat!" Maude huffed.

"They're an hour ahead of us." Ruby explained.

"Oh," Opal said as she contemplated such a complex concept. "Weird."

"That means it's already nine thirty there," Ruby said looking at her watch.

"Oh, well, then it's probably Georgia time then," Opal shrugged.

"You mean we've only got an hour and a half to get there?" Maude yelled.

"Oh God, it's almost a two hour drive," Ruby lamented

"Not today it isn't," Maude said and slammed her foot to the floor.

"Pedal to the metal! Yeehaw!" Opal squealed.

"I'm not okay with this!" Ruby yelled as Maude's makeup bag hit her in the face.

"It won't last long! We'll be there in a little bit," Maude said as the Chrysler Plymouth Fury gained speed.

"This is half the fun, Ruby!" Opal yelled back. She was holding onto the leather handle above her head for dear life. Although she didn't share the same enthusiasm when their heads suddenly hit the ceiling. The Fury had temporarily left the road when Maude cleared a particularly steep hill at top speed.

"Sorry!" Maude yelled back at Ruby.

Ruby and the bags had shifted positions. She was now catty corner to the doors. "Dadgum it, Maude!" Ruby yelled. By the time she righted herself, Maude took a sharp curve and she was thrown to the other side of the car again. "If I ever get out of this metal contraption, I'm never letting you drive again" Ruby yelled from the backseat.

"Hey Ruby, did you bring your camera?" Maude asked.

"I packed it in one of the bags. Who knows where it is now! Can you slow down?" Ruby answered.

"We gotta make time!" Maude yelled back.

Opal, for her part, had lost a little bit of excitement about this drive as well. The longer they drove, the paler Opal got. On more than one occasion, she attempted to stomp on the imaginary brakes on the floorboard. The leather handle that she clung to was strained to the limits.

"I can try to change flights, Maude! You ain't gotta kill us in the process!" Opal yelled.

"No! We're getting on that flight if it's the last thing I do!" Maude retorted.

"It could very well be!" Ruby yelled. Maude wasn't listening to them at all. She was too busy passing a semi truck before the passing lane ended.

"There's a car coming," Ruby muttered from the backseat. Maude said nothing, but continued to speed up. "Maude, there's a car coming!" Ruby said again, this time a bit louder. Her knuckles were white as she gripped the headrest in front of her tightly. Maude still said nothing and kept her eyes focused on the road.

"CAR!" Opal yelled, stomping the nonexistent brake with every ounce of energy she could muster.

Maude swerved back into the right lane with inches to spare. Ruby and Opal clutched at anything close while they hyperventilated. It was too much. Ruby closed her eyes and tried to brace herself for the next death defying stunt.

"Maude? Please. There won't be a vacation if we don't get there in one piece!" Ruby cried.

"It's okay. We're almost there. I can see the signs for the airport now," Maude said triumphantly, pointing to the sign with the airplane up ahead.

"Thank the sweet Lord Jesus!" Ruby cried.

"Yeah. What she said," Opal agreed. She was still trying to keep down the piece of banana bread she had stuffed in her mouth while Ruby got situated in the back seat.

"It wasn't that bad. Y'all act like I was going to kill you or something," Maude said. She took the left turn as indicated on the sign, which sent Ruby and Opal tumbling one last time. Five minutes later they screeched to a halt in one of the designated parking spots.

Ruby looked at her watch. Thanks to Maude's erratic driving, they had actually made up the missed time. They could still make their flight if they hurried.

"Hurry up, Opal. Get out of the car," Ruby pushed the seat in front of her.

Opal still hadn't opened her eyes. "Have we landed?"

"Yeah, now we have to run if we're going to make it," Ruby said.

Opal took a deep breath and opened the door. Ruby pushed the seat forward and began handing Opal the bags from the back seat. Maude was unloading the trunk.

"Come on, Maude!" Opal called as she and Ruby set off for the ticket counter. Opal was carrying Maude's makeup case and her own backpack. Ruby was carrying two pillows and her purse.

"I'm coming," Maude called after them. She put her suitcase under her arm before picking up Ruby's and Opal's suitcases. Clearly they had packed too much for Opal. Her suitcase weighed a ton. By the time she made it to the ticket counter, Ruby already had the tickets in hand.

"Oh, there you are. We thought you had gotten lost. Put those on the belt. We've just got time to make it if we run," Ruby told her.

Relieved to unload the luggage, Maude complied happily. She shouldered her own backpack and took her makeup bag from Opal. Somehow she ended up with Opal's bag, too. She took the ticket from Opal and they all ran to the gate.

~Chapter Four~

"Opal! I can't run as fast as you!" Maude yelled after them.

"Come on, you ol' goat. We can't stop now!" Opal yelled over her shoulder. "Come on!"

Ruby slowed down to wait for her struggling friend. Maude was always bringing up the rear. By the time Maude caught her breath, they had already lost Opal in the crowd of people exiting onto the tarmac to board the plane.

"Come on, Maude. Who knows where she's gone off to!" Ruby yelled.

"I'm coming! She can't get far! I've got her ticket!" Maude replied.

Ruby and Maude finally caught up to Opal in the line to board. Maude slipped Opal her ticket and together the three of them found their empty seats near the back of the plane. Ruby slipped in next to an older gentleman who had already nodded off to sleep. Maude was stuck between two teenage boys who looked like they partied too long into the night with substances unknown. That left Opal in the last row closest to the bathroom next to an uptight looking grandmother in a fancy dress and glittering tiara who sat in the middle seat with an empty seat on either side of her.

"Well hello madame," Opal bowed. The woman rolled her eyes and stiffened her already tight lips. "Excuse me, pardon me. I'm just going to sit here by you if you don't mind."

Apparently the woman did mind. She put her large bag in the empty seat by the aisle and said she was saving it for her husband who did not like to sit by the window.

"Oh well, then I'll just slide over into this one," Opal smiled.

Ruby stifled a laugh and looked out the window onto the tarmac. This was really happening. She was headed to Italy with her two best friends. She was leaving Rhinestone and Jameson and all of her responsibilities behind. At least for a few weeks. This would be her first flight ever. She was more excited than scared. They were headed for a small layover in New York City first. Just long enough to switch planes before they headed to Frankfurt Germany and then to Naples. Opal had really outdone herself with the arrangements, minus the small hiccup of time zones this morning.

"Y'all ready for this?" Opal called out. Many heads turned towards her and she gave an excited thumbs up searching for her two friends. She tried to high five the lady next to her, but she refused to acknowledge the spunky and excited Opal.

"Your husband better hurry if he's going to make it," Opal chattered.

"He's right here," the woman replied stoically. She motioned to her large bag that was still in the open seat.

Opal was very confused. "Whatcha mean he's right in there?"

The woman glared at Opal and turned away from her. Opal thought it best to drop the conversation and looked for Maude and Ruby. She found the back of Maude's head three rows in front of her.

"Hey Maude! Maude! Are you ready for this?" she asked.

Maude shushed her quickly and turned to face the front. As the plane turned and headed toward the flight line, Maude felt her stomach lurch uncomfortably. She wasn't so sure about this flying thing. She sat up straight when the engines revved to full throttle. By the time the plane taxied down the runway, she was a light shade of green. The uneasy feeling continued as she was pushed back in her seat from the sudden upward movement.

"Oh dear God," she muttered hoping the bile wouldn't rise any further in her throat. Maybe it was a good thing she had skipped breakfast.

Ruby too felt the unfamiliar lurch when the plane left the ground. Unlike Maude, she looked out the window with a sense of renewed anticipation. This was it. No turning back now. From the back of the plane, she heard Opal yelling "Wheeeee." Opal's lust for life always made Ruby smile.

Opal's seat companion was too busy reading a magazine article to hold an interesting conversation, so Opal leaned over her seat to the man directly in front of her and asked where he was headed.

"New York City," he responded gruffly.

"Wow, me, too!" she exclaimed.

The stranger looked at Opal like she had two heads. "I'm only going to be there for a few hours. You know, business," she replied.

"What kind of business?" he asked, suddenly interested in a possible business connection.

"Oh, you know. Travel mainly," she responded. She kicked her feet restlessly and sighed. "I'm going international, now."

"International, huh?" he asked.

"Yea, you know, the usual," Opal said. She was getting very animated and accidently kicked the back of his seat a little too hard.

The man rolled his eyes and turned his back to her. The woman next to her had switched seats with her large bag and returned to her magazine. "So, what's your name there big fella?" Opal smirked. The woman hissed and pulled the bag closer to her seat. This was going to be a boring and lonely flight for Opal.

Maude looked over to the young man on her right. He was holding his hand up in the air and slowly moving it from side to side. "Whoa, dude. Look at this. It's like there are four of them."

The guy on the other side began to copy his friend. "Man, that's groovy, Dave."

Maude put her hand on her chest and swallowed hard. She really wanted to kill these two idiots, but she thought that might push her stomach over the edge.

Ruby leaned her head against the window. She was close enough to Opal to catch snippets of her conversation. Why was Opal telling this stranger that they were international travelers? Well, she guessed that after this trip they would be. There were going to be spending a couple of weeks in Italy, after all. By the end of the summer, they would be able to count themselves among the jet setting elites. The thought brought a smile to her face as she drifted off to sleep.

After two hours, the pilot announced that they were making their descent into New York. They would be landing in a few minutes. This flight had been the longest two hours of Maude's life. She grabbed onto the two armrests. This brought the immediate attention of the young men on either side.

"Hey, you okay, little lady? Peter and I got you," Dave said. He snuggled up closer to Maude and grabbed her arm.

"We'll keep you safe," Peter added. "You just hang onto us if we crash. We'll protect you," he giggled and slapped his knee in delight.

The plane bounced on a pocket of air. "I'm going to die surrounded by these two idiots,"

Maude thought, but she didn't pull away when they each reached for a hand to hold.

Opal stopped her rendition of "All Shook Up" to listen to the announcement from the pilot announcing their arrival in New York. She immediately started dancing in her seat, much to the chagrin of the lady near her. Apparently, Opal's dancing interrupted an in depth conversation the lady was having with her husband who seemed to reside in the bag on the seat.

"Can you please give us some privacy?" she snapped.

"Oh, don't mind me!" Opal replied cheerfully.

Maude grabbed onto the boys' hands a little harder with each air pocket the plane hit. When the aircraft made a sharp bank on the final approach, the three were fully embraced, holding onto each other for dear life.

"Wow! I knew you were feeling some kind of way!" the red haired Dave smiled. "In some cultures we'd be practically married by now!" Maude threw his hand down in disgust.

"Don't worry, honey. We got something we can give you for those nerves when we land," Peter offered.

Maude couldn't get off this contraption soon enough. But the wheels touching the ground brought one more embrace for the trio. She tried to stomp on imaginary brakes to help the plane slow down. It was unnecessary. By the grace of God, the plane slowed on its own and made its way safely to the gate.

"See, little lady. We made it safe," Dave assured her.

"How about we get to know each other a little better and take the edge off of those nerves?" his friend Peter asked.

Now that Maude was back on solid ground, she could almost feel her stomach settling down. It wasn't settled enough to kill them, but she felt certain she could make them wish they were dead if she had to.

"Maude can you get the bags from the overhead?" Ruby yelled over to her.

"On my way," she replied. Saved from an awkward encounter, she left the boys to their own devices.

"After you, my liege!" Opal stood up and bowed to her neighbor. The woman snatched her bag up and exited the plane as quickly as possible.

"Hope you two have a great time!" Opal called after the fancy lady. She wove her way through the crowd until she found Ruby and Maude waiting for her by the large doors. "We made it! I'm ready for round two!"

They were scheduled to have an hour layover in New York City, which gave them plenty of time to find their new gate. Once they arrived and found some empty seats in the waiting area, Maude started to nod off to sleep. The flight to New York had tuckered her out quickly.

Ruby looked across the walkway and saw a gift shop on the corner. "Maude! Look! A gift shop! Come with me!"

"I'm too tired, Ruby. You take Opal with you," Maude yawned.

"I don't know where she went," Ruby shrugged. She was too intrigued by the rows of t-shirts hanging in the window to give another thought to where Opal had scampered off to. The classic "I love NYC" t-shirts were calling her name.

"We lost Opal?" Maude said, suddenly awake.

"I think she went off to the bathroom or somewhere," Ruby said, brushing Maude's concern away.

Ruby hurried towards the gift shop and looked for her size in the white shirts.

"Two for one special goin' on today," the man behind the counter said.

She had to take advantage of that deal! She couldn't get herself one and not one for her friends. She selected two mediums and a small shirt. That left one more that she could get for free. She paused for a second and thought about who she could get the other one for. She might as well get something for Jameson. He had never been to New York, but he had always dreamed of going. Even if they didn't get back together, she could at least be nice enough to bring him back a small token. She found a large shirt that matched the other three and brought them to the front counter.

"Can I interest you in any of these?" the man asked. He pointed to a shelf behind him that held miniature snow globes and small figurines of the Statue of Liberty and the Empire State Building.

They were too cute to leave behind. Ruby bought one of each, a couple of extra rolls of film, and a magazine that showed all of the new construction going on around the city. David Rockefeller had already begun construction on a large complex in lower Manhattan. Ruby would just have to come back in a few years and spend more than an hour.

"Look Maude! I bought you a t-shirt!" Ruby announced. Maude had tipped over in her chair and was snoring loudly.

"What?" Maude yelled.

"I got you a shirt. If you stay with the bags, I'm going to go to the bathroom and put mine on. Then you can go and put yours on!" she said gleefully.

Maude nodded incoherently and fell back asleep.

Ruby found the nearest bathroom that didn't have a line. Much to her surprise, Opal was seated on the bathroom sink tweezing her eyebrows.

"Oh, hey Ruby!" she squealed. "Isn't New York grand?"

"Yes! Look what I found," Ruby said. She showed her the snow globes and mini statues. "I bought us some shirts, too," Ruby said and passed Opal the smallest one.

"How chic!" Opal smiled. She pulled off the buttoned shirt and slipped on the white shirt from Ruby. "I love it! Only one thing is missing. I need to find some of those big sunglasses. Come on Ruby. Show me the goldmine where you found these treasures!"

Ruby quickly changed into her matching shirt and led Opal back to the gift shop.

"Back again?" the man laughed.

Opal found the largest pair of sunglasses they had in stock and could not resist the miniature snow globes either. While she was trying on sunglasses, Ruby had found some candy for the next leg of the journey. She better get Maude some treats, too, since she was doing such a great job of watching the bags.

"I better buy some film. We wanna remember this trip forever," Opal told Ruby.

"I just bought some," Ruby told her.

Opal thought for a few seconds. "I'm getting some more. You can never have enough pictures," Opal said.

They found Maude asleep in the same chair. Opal shook her vigorously until she woke.

"What in the devil is wrong with you?" Maude hissed.

"We come bearing gifts," Opal said. She dumped a bag full of candy and sodas into Maude's lap.

"Ahh! What are you doing?" Maude yelled. She jumped up and some of the bags fell to the floor.

"Maude! Look what you did. We can't take you anywhere," Opal shook her head. "Put on your new shirt Ruby got for you and clean yourself up a bit. We're about to board!"

Maude snatched the shirt from Opal and shuffled to the bathroom.

"Goodness gracious! Always waiting on that woman," Opal sighed. "Let me see the camera, Ruby. I want to check it out while we're waiting on slow poke."

Ruby rummaged through her bag and found the camera buried at the very bottom of the oversized tote. She handed the camera to Opal who was thrilled with the idea of a new toy. Ruby gathered up the bags from the floor and set them into the vacant seat. Maude soon shuffled back looking rather spiffy in her new shirt.

"Here are the bags," Opal said. "I kept watch on them while you were gone."

"Thanks y'all," Maude muttered. "They go well with the bags under my eyes."

"We don't have time to discuss your makeup woes, Maude!" Opal yelled. "We've got to get onto Germany!"

Opal had already skipped off to the front of the line closely followed by Ruby. That left Maude, once again, to bring up the rear with all of the newly acquired bags. Maybe this flight would be better, Maude hoped.

∾Chapter Five∾

The seating arrangements on this next flight were just as bad as the flight to New York City in Maude's eyes. Opal claimed the first open aisle seat in the front row next to a rather handsome gentleman. Ruby found an aisle seat two rows behind Opal, leaving Maude to squish in between two heavyset German ladies five rows back.

Ruby's seatmate was an American serviceman who was heading off for his first duty assignment. He was a handsome young man and he cut a dashing figure in his uniform. He seemed a little nervous to be flying.

"How long have you been in the Army?" she asked him.

"About six months. I just got out of training," he replied.

"Oh, so is Germany where you're going to be stationed?" she prodded further.

"Yes, ma'am. I got lucky with this one. I've always wanted to see Europe," he replied.

"So have I. My friends and I are going to Italy for a few weeks," she informed him.

"That sounds really nice," he said.

Their conversation was interrupted by the stewardess in the aisle asking them to fasten their seatbelts.

"Where ya headed?" Opal asked the man next to her.

"Uh, Frankfurt," he said.

"Interesting," she replied. "Big plans this weekend?"

"Um, no. Do I know you or something?" he asked.

"Nope. At least, I don't think so. What's your name?' she asked.

"Huh? Daniel. What's your name?" he asked uncomfortably.

"Opal. You got someone special over in the motherland?" she asked.

"Uhh, what? I'm sorry, but what? I'm just going to Germany for business. What are you doing there? Who are you?" he asked. He was clearly flustered.

"I told you I'm Opal, silly. I'm headed to Italy on vacation with my friends," she smiled and batted her long eyelashes at him.

"Oh, that sounds nice. Do you know anyone in Italy?" he asked.

"Nope. I never seem to meet a stranger though," she laughed.

"Have you ever been to Italy?" he asked. "I've been a few times and…"

"I'm flattered, truly, but you're not my type. Now my friend over there," she started to say. She stood up in her seat and yelled for Maude.

"Hey Maude! This guy over here says he's good at business. You know what that means!" she winked. She gave Maude a thumbs up and grinned. Maude sank down even lower in her seat. Opal pulled Ruby's camera out of her bag and snapped a picture of the unsuspecting man. "Just in case!" she grinned.

"In case of what?" he asked. Opal smiled and tucked the camera back into the bag. "Maude's a real peach. You're gonna love her! She's a tad on the grumpy side now, but once you get past that, she's a real tiger. Grrr!" Opal pawed at his face playfully.

"Um, I think you have the wrong idea here," he started to say.

"Oh, I think I have the right idea," Opal winked at him.

"Look, you're crazy, lady!" he shouted. The man jumped up and grabbed his bag from underneath the seat.

"I'm sorry sir, the pilot has asked for everyone to find a seat and fasten your seatbelts," the stewardess said sternly. He returned to his seat next to Opal and grimaced.

"Look at you! Already trying to go sit next to her. Just you wait, we'll be on the ground in no time!" Opal smiled. "Hey Maude! I'm gonna keep him company for you!" Opal was back on her tiptoes in the seat.

"Ma'am, please sit down and fasten your seat belt," the stewardess said again in a huff.

"Whoa da!" the heavier woman said. She gripped Maude underneath her arms and lifted her back into her seat. Maude was wedged in between the two women tightly. If there was any turbulence on this flight, she may not feel it. The two women were speaking heavy German as if Maude was not sandwiched between them.

"Um, would you like me to move so you two can talk?" Maude asked. She stood up and motioned for the woman on the left to switch seats with her.

"Nein, nein!" she said. She took Maude by the shoulders and sat her squarely in the seat. "Hinsetzen!"

Maude could not move, even if she wanted to, once all of the seat belts were fastened. The woman on her right buckled Maude in securely without asking if she needed help. This was probably the safest seat on the entire plane. Maybe Maude could at least get some sleep on this flight. Once they landed in Germany, they had to hurry to their next gate to get on the plane to Naples. There would be no time to dawdle. Maude had to be well rested in order to corral Opal and Ruby.

"This is my sister Helga," the larger blonde woman said. "I'm Gertrude. You travel mit your friend, ja?"

"Yes, ma'am. My friends and I are going to Italy," Maude responded as she tried to get comfortable. There was little hope of that on this flight, sandwiched as she was between these two full figured ladies.

"Ah, ja. We go to Italien die ganze zeit," she said in a thick German accent. "We have a sister der. And we get the olives fresh from der baum."

"Fresh! Ja," Getrude echoed.

The two women changed back and forth between German and English. Maude was getting a headache already and they hadn't taken off yet. There was a strange smell coming from their bags underneath the seat. Maude could feel her stomach churning already. She could hear Opal up front entertaining her new found friend. As they moved closer to the runway, Maude's stomach lurched uneasily. The smell emitting from beneath the seat wasn't helping. No doubt about it, Maude did not like flying. She held on for dear life while the plane climbed higher and higher. Maybe if she just closed her eyes for a minute she would be ok.

"Sauerkraut?" Helga asked. She had pulled out a foiled wrapped plate and a plastic fork. When she unwrapped the foil, Maude held her breath. She shook her head and clutched her stomach.

"I'm good," she whispered.

"Oh, you need this! Calms the nerves!" Helga smiled. She ate a bite of kraut and scooped her fork back into the bowl. She shoveled the fork into Maude's pursed lips and Gertrude patted her on the back.

"Ja! Good for nerves!" Gertrude laughed.

Maude somehow managed to swallow the mouthful. She knew it was only a matter of time before it rose back up. The smell was enough to knock a grown man over. She was going to have to make it to the restroom fast. She fumbled with the seatbelt and jumped up.

"Ma'am! Please return to your seat. We have not been given the all clear just yet," the attendant said sternly.

Maude ignored her and slammed the restroom door.

Opal turned around just in time to see her friend flee to the bathroom. "Hold on, Maude! Help is on the way!"

Opal leapt over her neighbor's legs and ran down the aisle towards the restroom. She pounded on the door and shouted, "Let me in Maude!"

"Ma'am! Return to your seat now!" the attendant yelled sharply. Opal ignored her and continued to pound on the door.

"Ruby! Ruby can you hear me? Maude needs our help!" Opal yelled over her shoulder. The entire crowd of passengers were now fixated on this spectacle unfolding in front of them. Opal returned her attention back to the closed restroom door.

"Maude! I'm right here! Let me in!" Opal shouted.

"Go away!" Maude yelled.

Opal did not seem to take the hint. "Is there a doctor on board?" Opal shouted. "We need a doctor over here!" No one seemed ready to volunteer. "That's ok! Let me in Maude! I'm as good as it gets!" Opal continued to knock on the door. By this time, the flight attendants had made their way to the bathroom door and were pulling Opal's arm.

"Ma'am, please return to your seat!" they directed. Opal could tell this was about to get ugly.

"Maude! They're coming for us! Come out or let me in!" Opal shouted through the door.

"Go away Opal!" Maude shouted back.

The flight attendant hooked Opal underneath her shoulders and dragged her back to the front of the plane to where her seat was.

"Maude! They've got me! Save yourself!" Opal shouted. She was dragged past Ruby who hid her face from Opal and the flight attendants. This was almost too comical to bear. Maybe no one would realize that she was part of their group.

"Ruby! Save yourself!" Opal yelled and flung herself towards the row of seats. Ruby could have died on the spot from embarrassment.

"Ma'am! Stop resisting. This is insane!" the attendant yelled.

One flight attendant buckled Opal back into her seat, much to the dismay of the already annoyed man. The other attendant walked back to the restroom door and pounded loudly on the door.

"Ma'am! Come out now or we will be forced to either come in after you or land the plane and have you and your party escorted off!" she shouted.

Maude emerged a few minutes later looking as though she'd been hit by a truck. She staggered back to her seat where her new German friends were watching the commotion with a keen interest. Between their running commentary, they continued to eat large helpings of kraut, but now liverwurst had been added to the feast. One look at their lunch and Maude pushed past the flight attendant to reclaim her throne in the restroom. When Maude finally felt comfortable enough to leave the restroom, she was greeted by a line of people who looked desperate. She found the back of Ruby's head and kneeled in the aisle near her.

"Please switch seats with me. I can't take any more of that smell!" Maude begged.

"Now that you mention it," Ruby said, "It's starting to get to me, too. Try Opal."

Maude all but crawled down the aisle to Opal's seat and found her singing to the man next to her. He had his hands over his ears and looked to be in intense pain.

"Opal," she whispered. "OPAL!"

Opal stopped singing and looked around wildly. "Yes?"

"Down here!" Maude said. "You've got to switch seats with me. I can't take it anymore!"

"I knew it!" Opal cried. "Love at thirty thousand feet!"

Whatever color that was left in Maude's face suddenly drained.

"No! I just can't take the smell back there," Maude replied.

"Sure, sure. I don't need an excuse Maude. Love is all around, love is in the air," she crooned. "Gte it? Air!" She happily left her seat and motioned for Maude to sit down. She playfully bopped the man on the shoulder and said, "you lucky dog! Mind your manners. I'll be watching!"

Opal left the two lovebirds alone and found her new seat between the two German ladies. The two women welcomed her heartily and Opal smiled at them both. Maude had not been wrong though. The smell was overwhelming. She stood up and yelled towards the front of the plane at Maude.

"Wow, Maude! You sure made a mess of things back here. It smells awful! What did you eat back at the airport?" Opal shook her head and sat back down. "So, how's it going?" Opal asked the two sisters. She was sure they were going to be the best of friends.

Before the rest of the passengers knew it, Opal and the two sisters were singing as loud as they possibly could to Buddy Holly's "Peggy Sue." Opal had already pulled out the camera to document their performance.

"Oh my God. I'm going to have to kill her," Maude mumbled to no one in particular. Her stomach had finally started to settle down. Maybe now she could doze off for a few minutes.

"Your friend is, um," he cleared his throat loudly, "something else."

"You have no idea," Maude responded. She could feel her eyelids getting heavier by the minute.

"You need to get her seen about," he said. "You can smell the crazy coming off of her. I'm surprised they let her fly without a straightjacket."

Maude opened her eyes and snapped angrily, "Don't talk about my best friend like that. There ain't nothing wrong with her."

Maude closed her eyes and left the man sitting there bewildered. Her peaceful nap was interrupted twenty minutes later when the stewardess came over the intercom requesting all passengers fasten their seatbelts. They were running into some bad turbulence. Maude's stomach was not going to catch a break today.

⸻ Chapter Six ⸻

"That was the best flight I've ever been on!" Opal cheered. She linked arms with Ruby and turned around to Maude behind them. "Come on, Maude! No time to dawdle."

Maude staggered off the plane, forcing a questionable burp down. She held onto the door for support. Helga and Gertrude caught up with her easily and handed Maude a small covered dish.

"Ah, Fraulein. You better, ja?" Helga asked, shifting her bags from one shoulder to the other. Once again the demon smell was awakened, but by now, Maude had nothing left to give back.

"Ja. You should eat the kraut like we say. You feel better," Gertrude added.

Maude swayed for a moment. "No thank you," she managed to say with effort. Gertrude snatched the covered dish back from Maude and looked annoyed.

Helga had seen Opal. "Opal! Fraulein Opal," she called ahead.

"Ah, our friend Opal. Yoo hoo. Opal," Gertrude followed her sister.

"You forgot your liverwurst and kraut!" Helga called.

"I'm going to have to kill them all," Maude whispered to herself.

"Oh, Helga! Gertrude! You almost let me forget!" Opal called back to them.

"Nein. Nein. We don't let you leave. We have all the time to help," Gertrude smiled sweetly.

Maude wasn't sure how much more of the smell she could take. "Thanks, but we can manage," she said.

"Nein, we help! Your German not so good," Gertrude said to Maude.

Ruby had to agree with that and smiled back at the two sisters. Maybe they would make their next flight on time after all. The two sisters helped them get their suitcases and luggage and led the way through customs chattering in German with Opal. Ruby had not been aware that Opal spoke even a little German, so she was pretty surprised. Opal really was always full of surprises after all. She looked around for Maude and found her lagging behind.

Maude was bringing up the rear with her arms full of bags. Somehow Ruby had managed to escape the plane with only her pillow and two bags of New York souvenirs. Opal was now carrying a small container of liverwurst that her new friends had given her.

"C'mon Maude, if you make us late for the next flight, I won't share this feast with you!" Opal laughed. Opal got their tickets for the next flight with help from Helga. Gertrude took the suitcases and luggage from Maude and loaded them onto the belt.

"We're good to go! Grab those remaining bags Maude and hurry up," Opal said.

"That's it!" Maude shouted. She threw down all of the bags and stomped her foot in the middle of the crowd. "I'm done! Carry your own bags!"

Maude sat down in the middle of the floor and refused to budge. Ruby looked horrified and Opal shook her head. "You can't take her anywhere," Opal said to Ruby. "Come on now. We don't have time for this. I'll help you carry some of this and Ruby will, too."

Opal loaded up Ruby's arms with bags and grabbed the pillow that had fallen from Ruby's arms. "Come on Maude. You ain't gotta make a scene about it," she said seriously.

Opal pulled Maude to her feet and pushed her along the crowded concourse. She pushed the covered dish into Maude's arm and guided her through the crowds following close behind Gertrude and Helga who kept pointing out different signs.

Maude held her breath and followed the group down the corridor without the slightest idea of where she was going. Ruby, for her part, was desperately trying to stop at every gift shop along the way. At one point when Maude looked over her shoulder, Ruby was nowhere to be seen.

"Come on, Ruby," Maude yelled.

"What?" Opal yelled.

"Ruby's gone!" Maude huffed.

"I can't take much more of this Maude. You're in charge of Ruby! I'm trying to get us to the plane!" Opal sighed.

Maude had some choice words for Opal, but she swallowed them along with the bile that rose every time she got a whiff of food she was holding.

"Y'all wait one cotton pickin' minute. I bet Ruby's in that dadgum gift shop again!" Maude grunted.

"You have a rough trip mit your friends, ja?" Helga asked Opal.

"Ja, they don't travel well. They, how you say, vereuckt? They are crazy, no?" Gertrude said to Opal with sympathy.

"You have no idea," Opal agreed, shaking her head.

Maude found Ruby in the back of the gift shop with her arms full of shirts and postcards.

"Damn't Ruby! We don't have time for this! Come on," Maude growled.

"I have to pay for this. Won't take but a minute," Ruby replied. She made her way to the counter and added a few handfuls of German candy to the total. She took the two plastic bags from the cashier and skipped back outside to where Opal and the German ladies were waiting. The bags were piled up at their feet.

"Off we go!" Opal said.

"I'm getting too old for this," Maude said to herself. She gathered up the bags and traipsed after the gaggle of women ahead of her. Opal and her new friends were leaving Maude to gather up the backpacks, bags, pillows, and whatever else was in the pile.

"Don't you dare!" Maude shouted at Ruby. Ruby had started to duck into yet another gift shop along the way, but Maude's shrillness scared her back into line.

"Maude! Ruby! Y'all hurry up now! We've only got twenty minutes to make our flight!" Opal yelled back at them.

Maude and Ruby looked at each other abruptly. "Did she just say twenty minutes?" Ruby asked.

"We need to hurry," Maude said. "If you could just take some of these bags and," Maude started to say, but Ruby had already caught up with Opal leaving Maude alone. Maude gritted her teeth and powered through the migraine that had begun to set in. She quickly adjusted the bags and set off at the fastest trot she dared. She could still see Opal and Ruby up ahead. As long as she could keep them in sight, she'd be okay.

Twice Opal had grabbed Ruby by the arm and led her away from the temptations of the airport vendors. These momentary pauses gave Maude the opportunity to catch up a bit. All and all, she was quite proud of herself, until she misjudged the bags' clearance and took out three nuns with one poorly timed turn.

"Ow!" Maude yelled. Her yell caught the attention of Opal, Ruby, Helga, and Gertrude.

"Apologies Sisters!" Opal called out cheerily. "Maude'll pray extra good tonight or something like that."

Ruby clutched her pearls and hurried along behind Opal ignoring the crowd that had gathered around the fallen nuns. Maude stepped over the pile of holy women and without a backwards glance took the lead.

"Nein! Wrong way," Helga huffed. She pushed Maude to the back of the throng and continued to lead the way.

"Hurry," Gertrude yelled. "They are boarding the plane!"

"Out of the way! We're coming through!" Opal led the charge. She hugged Gertrude and Helga tightly and promised to meet up with them as soon as possible.

"Rhinestone," she said slowly. "You can't miss it on the map!" She disappeared with one final wave. Ruby followed Opal and left Maude with the bags struggling to squeeze her way past Gertrude and Helga.

"You!" Helga held her hand up. "Eat more!" she commanded Maude who had tried to slip past the two women. Before Maude could utter a response, both sisters had gripped her in an overwhelming bear hug. Fortunately, there wasn't anything left for them to push out.

Maude broke free and found an empty seat next to Ruby. "Oh thank God!" Maude sighed. She sank into the empty seat and yawned. "I'm about to pass out."

"Are you feeling better?" Ruby asked Maude.

"A bit," Maude said. "I'm hoping this flight is just long enough for me to get a good nap."

Maude briefly heard the stewardess saying something in German. Probably the same safety briefing they'd heard twice already. No matter, they already knew all that. Ruby nodded and tucked her backpack underneath her seat. She wedged her pillow against the window, buckled her seatbelt, and closed her eyes. "Wake me up when we're close," she told Maude.

"I'm going to sleep, too!" Maude replied. "Opal can wake us up. Where is Opal?"

"Right here!" Opal squeaked. Maude turned to see Opal's head peer up from behind the seat. "I'll be sure to wake you as soon as we get there. Never fear Maude! Opal is here!"

"That's what I'm afraid of," Maude sighed and rolled her eyes.

"Oh, just go to sleep. You get so crabby when you don't get enough sleep. Me and what's your name?" Opal asked the man next to her.

"Amir," the man replied with a thick accent.

"Me and Amir here are gonna get along just fine," Opal smiled at her seatmate.

Maude felt bad immediately for Amir, but Opal was his problem now. Maude put her dark sunglasses on and leaned her seat back and immediately dozed off.

The flight attendant got to Ruby and Maude's row and asked Maude to put her seat back into the upright position. There was no response from Maude.

"Maude! You can't do that. Maude?" Opal tried to stand up, but Maude's seat was practically in her lap. "Maude!" Opal shouted.

Maude did not respond, so Opal did the only thing she knew to do. She swiftly kicked the back of Maude's seat, which snapped Maude's neck in a fierce sense of whiplash.

"What the hell!" Maude yelled. "She's trying to kill me!"

"I ain't trying to kill you, but you can't break the rules like this. It ain't all about you Maude!" Opal sassed back.

Ruby continued to snore, not realizing her two best friends were feuding right next to her.

"Madam, you must put your seat forward," the flight attendant told Maude.

Maude glared over her shoulder at Opal, but she complied with the stewardess' request.

"I'm going to kill Opal, yet," she said through gritted teeth.

The stewardess, satisfied that procedures were being followed to the utmost, left the two young women to settle their own disagreement.

"Now go back to sleep, grumpy pants!" Opal said. She turned to Amir who was slightly amused by this spectacle and jumped back into their conversation.

The takeoff was smooth and Opal was thankful that her two friends were getting some rest. She had their itinerary packed once they set foot in Naples. The flight shouldn't be more than a few hours long, which gave Ruby and Maude plenty of time to get their beauty rest. She was not above leaving them at the hotel if they couldn't get a check on their attitudes.

Opal had talked Amir's ear off until he too fell asleep, leaving Opal to entertain herself. She had already done her crossword puzzles and played all of her road trip games by herself. She was getting restless. She started kicking her feet to the beat of the song that was stuck in her head.

"Ow!" Maude howled. "Opal, quit it!" Her shouting woke up Ruby.

"Sorry! You've been asleep long enough. I'm bored," Opal whined.

"How long have I been asleep?" Maude asked while yawning.

"Couple of hours, I think," Ruby said. She stretched her long arms and accidently knocked the sunglasses off of Maude's face. "Oh, you might want to put those back on." She handed Maude her sunglasses and looked out of the window. The sun was shining bright and the clouds looked picturesque.

"We should be landing soon then," Maude said. She looked around and noticed that most everyone else was either asleep or reading. "Can you see anything?"

"Not really," Ruby replied.

"Shouldn't we be landing soon?" Maude asked again.

"I thought so, but we don't seem to be getting any lower," Ruby told her.

Maude flagged down the stewardess as she was passing. "Ma'am, when are we landing?"

The stewardess looked at her oddly. "Landing? We have nine hours before we land."

"Nine hours? How long is this flight?" Maude asked.

"It's almost thirteen hours, madam, but don't worry. The captain has said we're making very good time. We should arrive a little ahead of schedule," she smiled.

"How is it thirteen hours to get to Naples?" Maude demanded.

"Naples, madam? This plane isn't going to Naples. We're on our way to Kathmandu in Nepal," the stewardess explained.

"I beg your pardon?" Maude said.

"We are going to Nepal, madam," the stewardess said a little more pointedly. She wondered why this seemingly intelligent woman didn't know where she was going.

"Nepal?" Ruby asked, clutching her chest.

"Yes, madam. We are going to Nepal. As I already explained to your friend," she reiterated.

"OPAL!" Maude and Ruby yelled.

"What?" Opal popped up like clockwork in the seat behind them.

"She says we're going to Nepal! Not Naples! What have you done?" Ruby gasped.

"Oh. Well, that's weird. Same letters, so easy mistake," Opal shrugged.

"I'M GOING TO KILL YOU!" Maude hurled herself over the back of her seat and fell into Opal's lap. Amir woke with a fright.

∽Chapter Seven∽

"I MEAN IT! I AM GOING TO KILL YOU!!"
Maude yelled.

"Maude no!" Ruby yelled. She grabbed onto
Maude's kicking legs and held on for dear life.

"I mean it! She sent us halfway around the
world. I'm going to finally do it!" Maude flailed
across the back of the seat trying with all her might
to reach Opal's neck.

Opal, who had been showing Amir the fine art
of pressure point massage, used him to her
advantage. He was yanked out of his seat and
thrust in front of Maude where he caught a strong
left hook to the cheek. Neither Opal nor Maude
were letting go of the poor fellow. He was trying to
fend off both women without receiving another
punch to the face.

"You're going to hurt him Maude!" Ruby shrieked. She was still holding onto Maude's feet, but Maude was too strong for her. Maude managed to kick her way out of Ruby's grasp and tumbled to the floor in front of Opal's seat. Amir fell on top of her desperately trying to catch his breath.

"What fresh hell are we in?" the attendant squealed.

Opal leaned closer to the airline attendant and whispered, "She must not have gotten her nap out. She gets real cranky when she doesn't get her sleep."

The airline attendant looked at Opal like she had two heads.

"Hmm. Come to think of it, do y'all have any food around here. She gets even crankier on an empty stomach," Opal sighed. "She needs all the help she can get taking care of herself. That's why she has me."

"Should we throw some water on them?" the other attendant asked.

"You better put some liquor in there somewhere!" Ruby added. "This ain't going to be fixed with water!"

"Get up off of me!" Maude yelled. "And don't put your hands there!"

"Oh, I am sorry madam," Amir stuttered. He was having a lot of trouble pulling himself up in such a cramped space.

"Maude, you lucky thing. I think he likes you! We're going to find you a man yet!" Opal said, staring down at her friend.

"I swear to God Almighty I'm going to kill you!" Maude said.

"Well, we're closer to heaven than we've ever been!" Opal sang cheerfully.

Ruby stared at Opal and shook her head. "One of these days, Opal, I'm not going to be able to help you."

"Ma'am, you need to get up off the floor," the stewardess told her.

"I'm trying, but he won't get off!" Maude was kicking and swinging her arms with all her might. Every time Amir would try to move off her, she kicked or hit him again. His eye had already begun to turn a nasty shade of purple and he was hunched over in pain holding his groin.

"Amir and Maude, sittin' in a tree. K-I-S-S..." Opal sang in a high pitched voice.

"Opal, hush up with that nonsense!" Ruby told her.

"What?" Opal looked over at Ruby innocently. "I won't stand in the way of fate."

"I swear to God!" Maude said through gritted teeth. She finally tossed Amir off of her, much to his relief. "One of us has got to die and it might as well be her!"

"So does that mean I won't be the maid of honor?" Opal asked, confused.

Ignoring Opal, Ruby turned towards Maude who was still fuming in a crumpled heap on the floor. "Now Maude, there's really no reason to get upset. There's nothing we can do about it now." Ruby tried to be diplomatic.

"No reason to get upset! No reason to get upset? Ruby, we were supposed to go to Italy. We're going to Nepal!" Maude explained. She staggered to her feet, but she was so mad she couldn't even look at Opal at the moment. Wrestling with Amir had taken some of the fight out of her.

"I know. I know," Ruby said quietly.

"It'll be fine, Maude. Don't worry. We'll just catch a taxi or something back to Italy," Opal explained patiently. She rolled her eyes at Maude's constant habit of over reacting to such minor things.

Ruby, Maude, the flight attendants, and Amir all stared at her blankly.

"Catch a cab?" Maude yelled. "You want us to catch a cab from Nepal to Italy? There ain't a cab to goes from Nepal to Italy. It's in two different countries! Hell, THEY'RE ON TWO DIFFERENT CONTINENTS!"

"Oh," Opal pondered this new information. "Well, I guess we'll need to fly back or something if it's that big of a deal."

"That big of a deal?" Maude shouted. "That big of a deal!" Maude fished in her pocket for her cigarettes.

"Well, it ain't like you can walk very far in your condition," Opal replied.

"In my condition?" Maude glared at her.

"You know you, you get winded easy now. It's hard for you to keep up with me and Ruby. We had to keep waiting for you in the airport. Almost missed our connecting flight," Opal said

"What in tarnation are you talking about? I ain't pregnant?" Maude yelled.

"And you ain't gonna be with that kind of display you just showed. You should be really embarrassed," Opal declared. "That's no way to treat a fine young man who was so obviously interested in you." Opal smiled at Amir and patted him on the back.

Amir looked from one woman to the other. He was still trying to protect himself from the angry woman. He backed a few more feet away from Maude pushing himself as close to the window as possible, lest she attack again. He was still not sure how he got roped into any of this. He had been minding his own business and a tiny woman had plopped down next to him. He had fallen asleep somewhere in the middle of their conversation, only to be violently awakened by a choke hold out of nowhere. His book had been abandoned, lost somewhere in the scuffle with the bespectacled woman. The smaller woman was talking circles around everyone else and his head was already spinning. Though that could be from the melee he had just survived.

"Ma'am? What can we do about this issue? Is there anything the pilot can do?" Ruby asked the attendant sweetly.

"The pilot? Absolutely not!" she barked. She had had more than enough of these three Americans on board. "Are you asking if we can just turn around and drop you three off at your destination? Because that would be absolutely absurd!"

Opal mulled over her words and asked, "Got any parachutes?"

"If you don't sit down and shut up right this instant, I will personally push you out of the door!" the attendant barked at Opal. "Right there. Fasten your seatbelt and I don't want another word out of you for the remainder of this flight." Her dark eyes flashed and Opal sank down in shame.

"And as for you," she pointed at Maude. "You sit down, buckle up, and keep your hands in your lap like a child. I don't want to see you lift one finger until I personally unbuckle you when we land," she ordered.

Before she could scold Ruby, Ruby sank down and buckled herself in and looked straight ahead. Satisfied with that, the attendant changed her tone and softened her glare towards Amir. She asked him to retrieve his bag and she immediately upgraded him to a first class seat far away from the three women who were probably escaped inmates or mental patients. For an injured man, Amir moved quickly.

The other passengers were left in a stunned state of confusion over the brouhaha they had witnessed. How could it be that these young women didn't know where they were actually heading? It seemed unfathomable to most, but the intensity of the feisty woman's reaction seemed to be genuine. Perhaps they really were going to Nepal by mistake.

When the flight attendant ventured to the other side of the plane to serve drinks, an older man who was sitting across the aisle from Maude, leaned over and tapped her on the arm.

"Excuse me, but I think you might need this more than me," he said kindly. He handed her two tiny bottles of Jameson whiskey, an empty plastic cup, and a can of coke.

She smiled over at him. "Thank you," she said. She was careful to reach over to take the drinks so that she could avoid the eagle eyed stewardess who kept glancing in their direction every few minutes.

"Maude, she told us not to move," Ruby whispered. She shot the man a harsh look and he merely smiled.

"Hush Ruby. This is medicinal!" Maude snapped. Maude poured a smidgen of coke in the plastic cup before emptying one of the bottles of whiskey.

"You're going to get in trouble," Ruby whispered again, looking over at the stewardess. "Jameson? Really Maude!"

"I can't help what he gave me!" Maude retorted.

"Hey! I thought we weren't talking about him on this trip," Opal whispered loudly between the cracks of the seats.

"Shh, Opal! No one's talking about him," Ruby said. "Let's just make the best of all this and enjoy the rest of the flight."

"What are they going to do? Land the plane closer to where we actually want to be?" Maude asked her.

Ruby shook her head as Maude took the mixture down in one gulp.

"You want this one?" Maude offered the second bottle of whiskey to Ruby.

"No, I'm not getting that lady mad at me again!" Ruby shook her head earnestly.

"More for me then!" Maude said as she recreated the concoction which she downed in one gulp. Seconds later she smacked her lips with a much more contented look on her face.

"Thanks. I really needed that," she said the gentleman across from her.

"You're most welcome," he smiled. When the stewardess looked his way, he waved to her to come by. For a moment, Maude thought Ruby might have been right and they were really about to get in trouble, but the gentleman simply asked for more whiskey which he covertly handed to Maude once the flight attendant walked away.

After Maude's fourth drink, she found out his name was Reginald and he worked with a British firm in international trade. Two drinks later, she was offering to meet him after they landed in between singing a myriad of Elvis songs. Reginald smiled warmly over at her.

"I'm sure we can arrange something," he leered at the young woman.

"No we cannot!" Ruby scowled. "She will not be meeting you anytime or anywhere. Now that's enough. Don't you dare give her anything else or I'll call them back over here!"

"Laaaaa baam, baaaaam, baam, baa…" Maude hummed away.

Dear God! Now Ruby was going to have to babysit Opal and Maude. This was becoming too much.

"Baa, baaa, baa, bum..." Maude sang happily.

"Yes, Maude. You just go to sleep now and when you wake up we'll be on the ground," Ruby patted her arm gently.

"Okay. La, la, la, la baa, bum," Maude stammered, but she did close her eyes. A few minutes later, her incoherent song lyrics were replaced by the sound of rhythmic breathing. She was finally asleep.

The remainder of the flight passed uneventfully. Ruby really had to go to the restroom, but her fear of the attendant's wrath was not worth risking a quick trip to the on board bathroom. Maude snored soundly in her seat. Opal, meanwhile, had already been to the restroom twice and at one point across the aisle pointing out shapes in the clouds to an elderly couple who were thoroughly entertained by her.

"This is the best trip we've ever taken!" the man exclaimed happily. His wife nodded and clapped.

"I warned you!" the attendant roared. She grabbed Opal by the arm and drug her to the very front of the section. She personally buckled Opal into the jump seat and moved the empty snack cart in front of her so she could not escape. "This will be your last warning. If you ever want to fly again, I suggest you take it to heart."

Opal passed the time counting the beeps and noises that the plane and passengers emitted. Every few minutes she would ask any passing attendant how much longer their trip would be. At least they were getting closer.

When the pilot came over the intercom to announce that they would be landing soon, Opal let out a loud cheer. She was silenced by the glare of the passing attendant who checked for the hundredth time that she was still securely buckled.

∽Chapter Eight∽

"That was fun!" Opal said. She skipped along carrying the oversized pillow and a stuffed animal she had picked up along the way. The English couple she had befriended on the airplane hurried along behind her clapping their hands. She waited for Ruby and Maude at baggage claim.

Ruby held onto an unsteady Maude who was loaded down with all of the bags. Her nap on the long flight had sobered her up some, but the lingering effects of the alcohol had calmed her down significantly. She was smiling and flirting heavily with Reginald who had been stuck to her like glue once she woke up from her long nap.

"Maude, come on!" Ruby hissed. "Sir! Take your hands off my friend and kindly leave us alone." Ruby shook Reginald off and made sure she kept her eye on the obnoxious stranger.

"Opal! Get back here!" Ruby yelled. Opal turned around to see Ruby and Maude lagging behind yet again.

"I don't have all day, Rubes! Y'all come on!" Opal called back to her. She was off yet again, mixing into the crowd of locals and travelers.

"All day for what? We don't even know where we're going, Opal!" Ruby yelled into the sea of strangers. She looked around and realized that Maude had wandered off and she was left alone in a crowd of people speaking languages she had never heard before.

"GREAT! This is just great!" Ruby yelled.

"Can I be of service?" Reginald whispered. Ruby jumped a mile, shaken by his sudden intrusion. He had one hand on Maude's waist and Maude's suitcase in his other hand.

"No thank you!" Ruby snapped. "And I'll take that!" She snatched the suitcase from his hand and glared at him.

"I couldn't help but overhear that you're in a spot of trouble. You need to get to Naples, don't you? Or was that little display on the plane just for entertainment?" Reginald smirked and took Maude by the hand. He led her towards the ticket counter.

Ruby fumed. She took a deep breath, interlocked her fingers, and stretched her arms in front of her. She cracked all of her knuckles before she followed behind them frowning.

By the time she caught up with Reginald and Maude, Reginald was in a full blown argument with the man behind the counter. Maude stood next to him frowning and beckoned Ruby over. Opal was nowhere to be seen.

"It appears that the next available flight to Italy isn't for two days. Which means that you three ladies have the opportunity to explore this wonderful country," Reginald smiled hopefully.

"Are you sure?" Ruby demanded. "I thought you said you could help us."

Ruby turned to Maude. "This is what you get for trusting a man who drinks Jameson!"

"There's nothing wrong with Jameson!" Reginald said.

"Actually there's a lot wrong with Jameson," Maude hiccupped.

Ruby and Reginald both turned to Maude waiting for her to explain. Did she mean the whiskey or the man? Ruby wasn't sure she wanted to know.

Ruby shook her head and turned to the man behind the counter to discuss the flight arrangements to Italy. Unfortunately, Reginald was correct. There were no flights to Italy for a few days. She confirmed the tickets and turned to find Reginald's arm wrapped around Maude's waist once again.

"Now for the accommodations," Reginald said.

"Come on, Ruby," Opal said. "We got it from here, Reg."

Opal had suddenly appeared with all of their suitcases and luggage. Ruby was thankful for her sudden reappearance. At least tracking down Opal was now crossed off her immediate to-do list.

"I can take you ladies to a very nice establishment," Reginald offered. "I have a room waiting for me at…"

Ruby cut him off and shouted, "Good day, Reginald!"

"But," Reginald started to say. He reached for Maude's hand and was cut off by Ruby.

"You are not taking us anywhere! And get your hands off my friend! I said good day!" she huffed.

Opal looked from one to the other. The redness in Ruby's neck was quickly spreading up to her ears. Ruby didn't get angry often, but when she did, it was always for a very good reason. Ruby shot her friend a look as she tried to pry Maude away from the overly eager Englishman.

"Come on Maude. We gotta get you to the hotel," Opal said, taking her friend's other arm.

"But where are you staying?" Reginald asked. "I can easily find you a room near mine."

"Did I overhear you say you need a place to stay?" a young man suddenly interjected. "You have the most beautiful eyes I've ever seen," he said to Opal. "I couldn't help but notice them from all the way over there."

Opal blushed and murmured "thank you."

"My name is Kamal Gurung," he bowed. "And what is your name?"

"I'm Opal. These are my friends Ruby and Maude," Opal said.

"I know of a place," he said. "It may not be as nice a place as the Duke of London here was suggesting, but one where I take travelers often" he sneered.

"Here, here now! These beautiful ladies deserve better than what you can provide," Reginald said sternly.

The young man ignored Reginald and stared at Opal. "So, what do you say, blue eyes?" he asked.

"You are the charmer, aren't you," Opal laughed.

"Where did you drop out of the sky from?" he asked. "Who do I have to thank for this chance meeting?"

"Probably my uncle Frank," Opal laughed. "I mean, that's where I get these old blue eyes!"

"Frank? Blue eyes? You know Frank?" the young man asked excitedly.

"Of course I know the Frank!" Opal said. "He's my uncle." She rolled her eyes and twirled around in a circle. "One time we," she started to say before the young man cut her off.

"I can't believe he's your uncle? Do you think I could meet him one day?" he exclaimed.

Opal shrugged her shoulders and looked at Ruby. "I mean, anything is possible. He does love to travel."

"Well, this changes things! Come on then! I know a place fit for a king!" Kamal said. He had not heard anything that was said after the mention of the Opal's uncle Frank.

"Looks like we won't be needing you!" Ruby beamed. She took over the bags from Maude and followed Opal, Maude, and the young man who was zig zagging his way through the crowds.

"Do we even know where he's taking us?" Ruby wondered aloud.

"Hey! Where are we going?" Opal called after the young man.

"I've got the perfect place. Don't worry!" he called over his shoulder.

"No idea!" Opal said to Ruby. "Yamal said he's got it taken care of!"

"I don't think that's his name, Opal," Ruby replied.

"Well, it's something like that. Hey Yamal! Wait for us!" Opal shouted.

"Just follow me!" he replied. He led them outside to a busy street full of honking cars and bustling activities.

"Put your bags in here and you climb up in this one. My friend Shamar will take care of you," he said to Maude. "He'll follow me!"

"I don't know about this," Ruby muttered.

"It'll be fine. He's a nice guy," Opal beamed.

"You don't know if he's a nice guy or not. He could be a murderer," Ruby lamented.

"He doesn't look like a murderer. Hey, Mamal, are you a murderer?" Opal asked the young man.

Kamal looked stunned. "What? Oh no ma'am, Opal. I'm very nice."

"See Ruby, I told you he was a nice guy. He even said so himself," Opal was satisfied.

Ruby wedged herself in the rickshaw seat and Opal stuffed the pillows and remaining bags around her. "Here, hold onto this," she said as she shoved her purse into Ruby's arms.

"Where are you gonna ride?" Ruby asked Opal.

"Right here of course!" Opal said. She climbed behind Kamal on the small cycle seat and wrapped her arms around him. "Let's go!"

"I don't know about this!" Ruby squealed as the rickshaw shot into oncoming traffic. She could hear Maude cursing loudly behind her.

"Hold on tightly. Are you sure you won't be more comfortable in the back with your friends?" Kamal asked as he dodged cars on either side of him.

"Oh no, I'm going to help you drive," Opal announced proudly.

"Oh God," Ruby pleaded. She shut her eyes and refused to open them no matter how many times Opal yelled "WHEEEEE!"

It was worse than riding in the back of Maude's Plymouth Fury. Much worse. Ruby was thrown from side to side and once, during a rather sudden braking, in which Kamal barely avoided an oncoming car, Ruby was launched forward and almost unseated Opal from her perch. There were quite a few words exchanged at that point and Ruby was glad she didn't speak Nepali.

Maude had sobered up completely by this point. She was muttering under her breath about people who couldn't drive all the while searching for anything to grab on to.

Ruby couldn't take anymore. She braced as best as she could and closed her eyes once more.

Throughout her Baptist upbringing, she had learned that prayers were more sincere if your eyes were closed and there was never a better time to pray than right this very second.

"We're here, my Opal," Kamal choked. Ruby slowly opened one eye and saw Opal's arms wound tightly around Kamal's throat. Kamal extended his hand to Ruby, but Opal was still clinging tightly to his back like a small backpack.

"Opal, I think you're hurting him!" Ruby cried.

"What a thrill!" Opal yelled jubilantly. "That alone was worth the flight!" She released Kamal and landed gracefully on her feet. "Come on Ruby, we better go rescue Maude."

Ruby looked behind her to see Shamar and Maude pedaling in behind them. Maude was red faced and she was holding her stomach with her cheeks puffed. Kamal and Shamar began to unload the two rickshaws and brought the bags to the front of the hotel leaving Ruby and Opal to unload Maude.

"Come on, old gal!" Opal sang cheerfully. She tugged at Maude's crossed arms and managed to pull her out of the small rickshaw. "Feeling better?"

Maude shot her a dirty look and snatched her backpack and pillow from the rickshaw.

"The Mandapa Shangri-La," Ruby said in awe.

"I didn't know you spoke Nepali!" Opal said. "Don't worry, Maude. Me and Ruby will teach you." She patted Maude's arm and smiled.

"It's so beautiful!" Ruby cried.

Kamal and Shamar had finished unloading the rickshaws and carried the bags inside the hotel.

Kamal motioned for the three women to follow him. Once inside, he spoke to the man behind the counter in a low voice. He pointed behind him towards Opal and the man behind the counter smiled.

"Yes, yes! We can help! Mr. Frank, you, yes!" he exclaimed. He quickly rounded the counter and shook Opal's hand vigorously. Opal returned the handshake and bowed. The man clapped his hands and snapped his fingers. Two men suddenly appeared and began marching the suitcases and bags upstairs. Kamal motioned for the women to follow their bags and waved goodbye to Opal.

"If you need anything, my uncle will take care of it. He is honored to have such celebrities here at his hotel. Opal, I would love to see you again very soon," he explained.

Ruby and Maude looked perplexed, but Opal smiled and nodded.

"Thank you, Hamal!" she said.

Kamal looked confused, but accepted her crushing hug. This had certainly been an interesting outing.

Opal rushed to catch up with Ruby and Maude who were already rushing up the stairs after the two bearded gentlemen. Once they reached the top of the stairs, the first man pulled out a key on a long chain and unlocked the door.

"Right this way," he announced. Opal, Maude, and Ruby walked into the large room and their jaws hit the floor. They were going to be staying in the nicest room in the entire hotel. The man set the final bag on the floor just inside the door. "If you need anything, just ask for Mr. Magar."

He held his hand out and waited with a smile.

"Oh," Opal said. She pulled out the wad of chewing gum from her mouth and placed it in his outstretched hand. "I get it. No chewing gum in Nepal. Got it!"

She looked around at Maude and Ruby to make sure they weren't chewing any gum. The man turned up his nose and walked back down the stairs without another word.

"How come they put us in such a swanky place?" Maude whispered to Ruby.

Ruby waited until the man was out of the room and the door was closed tightly before she turned to Maude. "Because somewhere during the course of our journey from the airport to here, our driver got the impression that Opal is related to Frank Sinatra," she explained.

"Which Frank?" Maude asked in disbelief.

"You heard me. Frank Sinatra," Ruby replied.

"Oh good grief! The only famous person Opal is related to is Wilhelmina, the town psychic! And she's only famous because of that scandal with the commissioner and his wife. You know nobody ever did find out what happened, but I swear she put a curse on them!" Maude said firmly.

"Maude you don't really believe all that. She's just different. That's all," Ruby offered diplomatically.

"Different like a voodoo doctor. I'm telling you she put a hex on them," Maude said.

"Aunt Willie ain't a voodoo doctor, Maude. She just grows a lot of herbs and medication. She's a real hoot come Christmas time!" Opal said.

"Well, voodoo doctor or not, now these people think Opal is related to Frank Sinatra!" Ruby said. She didn't like to gossip.

"Hell, Opal's more likely related to an actual hotdog frank than Frank Sinatra! Jesus Opal, what's gonna happen when he finds out you're nothing but a loon!" Maude swore.

"I never said I was related to Frank Sinatra. I was telling him about the time me and uncle Frank went fishing over at Trout's Hollow. It ain't my fault he interrupted me," Opal shrugged. "Plus we ain't gonna be here for long. I'm already working on getting us back to Naples."

"What do you mean back to Naples?" Ruby asked. "We haven't made it there yet!"

"You worry too much Ruby. I've got it all under control. Mamal said a direct flight is all it takes to get to Italy. Or something like that. I say we take in the sights and enjoy a few days in Nepal, then we can make our way to the sandy beaches!" Opal said.

"You've got it under control? You're the one who didn't know the difference between Naples and Nepal," Maude reminded her.

"Look at all the fun we've had so far!" Opal pointed out. "You can't get cheap thrills like this in Rhinestone, that's for sure."

"You're right about that, Opal!" Ruby agreed. She dug through her backpack and pulled out a wrinkled shirt. "Here Maude, change into this."

She tossed Maude the off-white shirt that read "Ich liebe Deutschland."

"I ain't wearing that,"' Maude said without hesitation.

"But they're so cute!" Ruby gushed. "We can be triplets."

"But we're not identical," Opal said. "One of us is so grumpy. Guess which one!" She pointed at Maude who still had a sour look on her face.

Maude grunted at the unfairness of it all, but she put the wrinkled shirt on all the same.

⌒Chapter Nine⌒

The Mandapa Shangri-La was clearly the most expensive hotel on the street. Ruby liked the way the name of the hotel rolled off her tongue. "The Shangri-La, Shangri-La," Ruby sang. "We don't have this kinda thing back in Rhinestone."

Maude crossed her arms and sat on the bed. The new shirt was very tight and was already making her feel itchy. She was getting hungrier by the minute, but Ruby insisted she needed time to freshen up. Opal exited the bathroom and began putting on her makeup.

"Y'all! There's a darling little commode in here!" Ruby exclaimed.

Maude hurried to the small bathroom and peeked inside. "What's that bin for?" she asked Ruby.

"I don't know. Maybe a trash can," she reckoned.

"Let me get in there real quick," Maude said. She hurried in the bathroom and held the door open for Ruby when she was done. "Y'all hurry up," Maude said. She was getting restless and did not care about whether the toilet was cute or not.

Ruby rolled her eyes. Maude got cranky every time she got hungry. If they didn't find her something to eat soon, she was liable to start cussing. "Just give me a few more minutes," she said. "Y'all figure out where we're going and by that time I'll be ready."

Opal pulled out a tube of lipstick from her pocket and rolled it over her lips. She smacked her lips and declared herself to look perfect. "Alright, Maude, what's the plan?" Opal asked.

"I ain't never been to Nepal, Opal! Some city called catawampus or something like that probably don't have good fried chicken!" Maude huffed.

"As always I have to plan everything," Opal said, rolling her eyes. "Come on, let's have some fun! I'm sure I can scrounge up something to eat!"

Maude looked over at Ruby who was coming out of the bathroom wearing the same "Ich liebe Deutschland" shirt that Maude wore. "Opal, if I have to wear this damned thing then you've got to wear yours, too."

"Ok, I mean, when in Rome!" Opal said cheerfully.

"We ain't in Rome," Maude snapped. "All because you failed Geography!"

Ruby and Opal ignored Maude.

"We'll have to find us some Nepal ones while we're out," Ruby announced.

"Are we going to get a shirt from everywhere?" Maude asked Ruby.

"Of course we are!" Ruby said, surprised that there would be any confusion about that.

"We passed some cute little markets on the way here," Opal said. "I bet we'll find all kinds of things there."

"We better find something to eat. I'm wasting away over here while y'all ramble on," Maude huffed.

"We're waiting on you, grumpy guss!" Opal said. She pulled her shirt on over her other clothes. She gave off the air of a tourist gypsy with flyaway hair.

"I'm ready to go, too," Ruby said. "Where to?"

"Let's go to those cute little markets," Opal said. "Come on, Maude. I'm getting hungry." Before Maude could respond, Opal jerked her off the bed by her arm and ushered her out of the door to the staircase by their room.

"Should we take another rickshaw ride?" Ruby asked once they arrived in the lobby of the hotel.

"I ain't getting on another one of them things for the rest of my life!" Maude hollered. Opal rolled her eyes and started to walk out into the sunny street.

They soon discovered that life on the other side of the world was drastically different than the small town of Rhinestone. The streets were smaller, but somehow packed with twice as many people. Rickshaws and motorcycles zoomed by barely navigating the tight spaces between the outdoor shop displays and the hundreds of pedestrians who seemed to have appeared in the short time that they had been up in their room.

"Y'all remember where the hotel is, right?" Ruby asked as they turned left down a random street.

"Yeah, it's right over there," Opal said.

"She means when we get lost," Maude huffed.

"You worry too much, Maude," Opal said. She turned to see Ruby wander into the display of silk scarves.

"We're going to get lost," Maude grumbled. "Then I'll be hungry and lost."

"Oooh, I like these," Opal said to Ruby. "Look Maude, what do you think?" She held a brilliant maroon caftan up to her face.

"I'm hungry," Maude said. She stomped her foot and crossed her arms.

Ruby threw down the scarf she was holding. "Come on. Let's get some food before she dies of starvation," Ruby rolled her eyes. Maude looked to be on the edge of a full blown tantrum.

"That's the best idea I've heard all day," Maude said.

They wandered down narrow alleyways to a few more stalls in the market and finally saw a man behind a counter full of different kinds of breads. "This looks delicious," Opal cried.

"I ain't eating it," Maude huffed.

Ruby pulled Maude to the side. "Why not?" she whispered.

"I don't know what it is," Maude said.

"We can't be rude!" Ruby replied. "I'm sure it's fine." Ruby looked over her shoulder and saw Opal chatting and smiling with the Nepali man.

"Come on Maude," Ruby gently nudged her towards the counter.

"Alright, fine," Maude said. She lagged behind Ruby with a sour expression on her face.

"Here Maude, try this one," Opal said. She handed Maude a chunk of dark bread. "I can't stop eating it."

Maude hesitantly took a bite. "Hmmm. That's not bad," she admitted.

"Told ya!" Opal smiled. She grabbed up the rest of the bread they had purchased and they continued to wander down the street, stopping occasionally to let Ruby explore the merchants. "What's that?" Opal asked. She had turned to find another food vendor.

"Look! Pancakes!" Maude yelled happily. She hurried over to a stall that had bowls of different foods scattered across the counter. The woman behind the counter smiled and handed her a piece of what did indeed look like a pancake.

"This is great!" she exclaimed.

"What is it?" Ruby asked.

"A pancake," Maude said in between mouthfuls.

"Wo," the woman smiled.

"She said to slow down," Ruby cautioned.

"No, no," the woman replied. "Wo." She pointed to the sign directly in front of the basket.

"Oh, it's called wo," Ruby nodded. She smiled at the woman and asked about the other baskets present.

"Momos," the woman offered. She handed Ruby a small bowl with three pieces of what looked like dumplings in a red sauce.

"Thank you," she replied. She took a bite and was surprised at how good it tasted.

"Opal, come try this!" Ruby said.

Opal reached into the bowl with her finger and pulled one of the momos out. "That's amazing," she cheered. The woman behind the counter smiled and looked at Maude.

"I don't know about this," Maude said.

"Maude! Don't be rude," Ruby whispered. Maude slowly took the bowl from Ruby and ate the remaining momo. It was a little too spicy for her liking. She must have looked uncomfortable. The woman handed her a bottle of something from underneath the counter and she drank heavily from it.

"Oh God!" Maude said. She spit out a mouthful of the warm beverage and shook her head. "No thank you!"

She handed the bottle back to the woman who looked offended.

"Maude!" Ruby screeched. "What are you doing?"

"It's hot beer! I ain't drinking hot beer," Maude said.

"Tongba," the woman said. "Momos and tongba."

"What's in this?" Maude asked her and held up the bowl.

"Lamb," the woman replied. Ruby swore she saw a hint of a smile on the lady's face when Maude ran off into the alleyway to puke.

"Thank you," Ruby smiled at the woman. "It was all wonderful."

Opal bought a few different foods and a few bottles of rice beer before they went off to find Maude. By mid afternoon, they had eaten their fill of the various dishes Kathmandu had to offer. Maude stretched lazily. Now that she was full, the exhaustion from the trip was starting to set in.

"Just out of curiosity, does anyone know the way back to the hotel?" Maude asked as she looked around. She had completely lost count of the turns they had taken and she was afraid Ruby had as well. Opal, bless her heart, couldn't find her way out of a paper bag, so she was never any help with directions.

"Yeah, it's right over there," Opal offered, waving into the sky indiscriminately.

Ruby looked at Maude. "I thought you were keeping up with where we were going," she whispered.

"Everything looks the same here. I'm completely turned around," Maude admitted.

"Don't worry. We'll find our way back," Opal said happily. "Let's head this way. It's probably up here." Opal headed out into an open courtyard area that they hadn't been to before. "Oooh," Opal exclaimed. "Pretty."

Towering above everything around them stood a magnificent temple adorned in oriental carvings. "That's absolutely beautiful," Ruby gushed.

Maude, who had stopped walking, stood back and stared up in amazement. "What is this place?" she asked. They walked up to read the plaque on the wall.

"It's called the Taleju Temple," Ruby read the English translation. "Says it's one of the most important Hindu sites in the whole country."

"Hindu? Huh. I guess they don't have many Baptists around here, do they?" Maude muttered. She was still fascinated by the ornate craftsmanship of the carvings.

"Let's go in!" Opal said. She stormed up to the enormous wooden door and pulled on the round door handle. Nothing happened. The ancient door wouldn't budge.

"Opal, we can't go in there. We're not Hindus," Ruby told her in a hushed whisper. "You're gonna get us in trouble."

"Maybe we wanna convert," Opal said, looking for a secret panel that might unlock the door.

"We ain't converting to Hindu, Opal. Have you lost your mind?" Maude said gruffly.

"I'm just saying they don't know if we wanted to or not," Opal shrugged.

"We need to get out of here before you get us in trouble," Ruby repeated her warning.

"Come on," Maude shooed her away from the door.

"Well at least let's get a picture," Opal said.

"Fine, fine." Ruby pulled out the Kodak Colorsnap from her purse and they tried to ask a passing older gentleman in their best Nepali sign language to take their photo. After a few minutes, he seemed to understand enough to hit the button. There was no telling what that picture would look like once they got home and had the film developed.

"It's hot. We need to find something to drink," Maude said. She had finally dragged Opal away from the temple.

"Come on, I saw some drinks back here," Ruby said. She led them back through the marketplace they had come from until she found the vendor selling sodas.

"I'll take two of those. It might be awhile before we find anybody else selling them," Maude reasoned. Ruby bought two drinks for each of them.

"Maybe we should start to head back," Ruby suggested. "I'm getting kinda tired."

Despite her misgivings about the rickshaws, Maude's feet were beginning to hurt and she was longing for the comfort of the hotel bed. "Yeah, that's a good idea."

Even Opal, who was normally bubbling over with energy, looked a bit worn out.

"Let's go ahead and get on one of those deathtraps," Maude offered.

"How do we tell them where we want to go?" Ruby asked Maude when they climbed inside an available rickshaw several minutes later.

"Big hotel.Shangri-La," Maude said. She raised her arms above her head to indicate size. The driver gave her a toothless grin and nodded. They were off, bouncing around the streets of Kathmandu.

"This doesn't look right," Ruby mentioned to Maude after the fourth turn. They were out of the main part of the city now, heading up a hill.

Maude was too busy holding on for dear life to worry about anything else.

"Oooh, look! Monkeys!" Opal squealed. "I've always wanted a pet monkey!"

"Monkeys?" Maude asked no one in particular.

"Our hotel didn't have monkeys," Ruby said. "At least I don't think it did."

"It didn't have a gold dome either," Maude added.

"Where are we?" Ruby asked the driver.

He nodded vigorously. "Yes. Yes," he said, giving Ruby the same overhead hand signal that Maude had given him earlier.

"No. We wanted to go to our hotel," Ruby told him. She shook her head and waved her hands.

"Yes. Yes," he waved back.

Opal took off up the steep stone steps towards the temple.

"Come on, Ruby. We lost him somewhere in the translation," Maude tugged on her arm. "Now we gotta go find Opal. She has found her long lost friends swinging in the trees."

They could hear Opal taking the steps two at a time while calling for the monkeys to come closer.

Maude grabbed the bags from the rickshaw and paid the man before he pedaled off.

"Oh good heavens," Ruby said looking at her friend climbing to the heavens. "We gotta climb all those?"

"Maybe by the time I get to the top, I'll be too tired to kill her," Maude lamented.

"That's if we make it up there," Ruby added.

The two friends slowly followed after a squawking Opal. When they made it to the top of the stupa, Maude opened one of the bags to grab a piece of bread for herself. The climb up the steps had taken all of her remaining energy. Before she could eat the piece of bread, a monkey snatched it from her hand. "What the hell?" she snapped.

A swarm of monkeys crowded around her jabbering and pulling at her clothes. "Help me Ruby!" she yelled.

"Oh look! You made some friends!" Opal exclaimed, showing up from out of nowhere.

"Friends! Get these durn things off of me!" Maude yelled, swatting the beasts away from her food. She threw the two bags full of bread away from her and the monkeys scrambled after them.

"Get me out of here!" Maude cried. She ran down the steps surprisingly fast and could hear Ruby behind her.

"Wait for me," Opal yelled. "I'm trying to get this small one to come with us. If he'd only get in my bag."

"NO!" Maude and Ruby shouted at the same time.

Opal sighed and stomped loudly down the stairs after her friends. They always got to pick their favorite souvenirs, but they always seemed to draw the line at live animals. Maude and Ruby were waiting for Opal at the base of the staircase when she lumbered down the last step. Ruby wove her arm through Opal's arm so she wouldn't lose her again.

"Well that was fun, but now how are we going to get back to the hotel? I'm so turned around I don't know which way is up," Maude told Ruby.

"We can try another rickshaw," Ruby offered.

"We'll probably end up at another temple," Maude said.

"There can't be that many temples here," Ruby said.

"That's like saying there ain't that many churches in the South," Maude peered over the rims of her sunglasses at Ruby.

"Well, that's true," Ruby nodded.

Ruby still had her arm interlocked with Opal's. It was the only way to keep Opal from bounding back up the steps to adopt a new friend.

"I don't think we have much of a choice. Let's see if we can flag somebody down," Maude told her.

"What about Jamal?" Opal asked.

"Your new boyfriend who carried us to the hotel in the first place?" Maude asked. "We're never going to find him in all these people."

"I don't know why not. He's standing right over there," Opal said. She pointed to the cluster of rickshaw drivers huddled together. Standing in the middle of them all was Kamal, the only person in Kathmandu who actually knew where they were staying.

"Well I'll be damned," Maude said.

∽Chapter Ten∽

Maude had never been so happy to see a man in her life, even if this one had the wrong impression about who they were. She climbed into the rickshaw sandwiched in between her two best friends and they set off for the hotel. She would have liked to have dozed off during this joyride, but traffic laws seemed to be optional in this part of the world. She could feel her lunch threatening to escape with each bounce. She turned to Ruby who also looked a little worse for the wear. Opal was the only one who seemed completely unscathed by the jostling of the rickshaw through the afternoon chaos of the Kathmandu streets.

They thanked Kamal greatly when they reached the main entrance of the hotel. Opal gave him a great big hug and a kiss on the cheek before bounding up the stairs ahead of her friends. They were so relieved to be back at the hotel, but none of them were prepared for the sight that awaited them at the top of the stairs. Four men in white work clothes were gathered in the open door of their room immersed in a fierce argument.

Maude wasn't having any of this. She was too tired to entertain a party. "Can I help you?" she asked pointedly.

The men looked at her briefly before returning to their argument.

"Excuse me! I said, can I help you?" Maude said, much louder than the first time.

"Maude, be nice," Ruby reminded her.

"I am being nice. They're the ones in our room who ignored me," Maude corrected her.

Mr. Magar stepped from the huddle of men talking. "I'm sorry ma'ams. This room is closed. Bad. Bad. Very bad. The whole thing flooded."

"Flooded? How in the world did it flood?" Ruby asked.

"It's probably the thousand year old plumbing. Clay pipes don't last forever, you know," Opal offered sagely.

Mr. Magar looked at her with a confused expression on his face. "No. No. The bathroom. All clogged. Bad. Bad. Very bad," he said painfully.

"Who's been in our room that flooded the bathroom?" Opal demanded.

Mr. Magar bit his tongue and shook his head. He ignored the three women and returned his attention to the men. Maude took control before anyone said anything else. "I'm sure we'll be moved to another room, perhaps one without any plumbing issues," she said with more confidence than normal.

"Yes. Yes. Of course," Mr. Magar nodded. He snapped his fingers and two young men hurried up the stairs. He yelled instructions that neither Maude, Opal, nor Ruby understood, but he did so forcefully. The young men had all the bags in their arms while Mr. Magar showed the ladies to their new room.

Once all the men were gone and the girls were safely settled into their new room, Maude turned to Ruby and asked, "How did you break the bathroom?"

"I didn't break the bathroom," Ruby said defensively.

"Well, it was fine when I was in there after Opal. You were the last one in there, so it had to be you," Maude said directly.

"She probably flushed the toilet paper down the commode," Opal said, emerging from the bathroom.

"Of course I flushed the toilet paper down the commode. What else are you supposed to do with it?" Ruby asked.

"Throw it in the trash," Opal replied as if that was the most natural thing she'd ever done.

"Throw it in the trash?" Ruby asked. "That's nasty."

Maude gasped and wrinkled her nose.

Opal shrugged. "That's what the sign said."

"What sign? There wasn't a sign in that bathroom," Ruby huffed. She stormed past Opal and went to find this sign Opal was talking about. A few seconds later, a very ashen Ruby came out holding the sign that clearly explained that the plumbing couldn't handle toilet paper the way that European and American plumbing could.

"Told ya," Opal shrugged.

"Oh my goodness, Maude. It was my fault that the room flooded," Ruby showed Maude the sign.

"That's weird," Maude said as she read the notice. "I guess I didn't see the sign either. Oh well."

"Do you think we should tell them about this?" Ruby always worried about doing the right thing.

"Not right now, I don't. You saw how mad everybody was," Maude advised.

Ruby bit her lip and Opal laughed. "Glad it wasn't me," Opal smiled.

"Listen, we're all beat from the trip over here. We're hot and tired. Let's get our baths and get some sleep and then we can decide whether or not to tell him about this," Maude suggested.

Ruby nodded. "Okay, I just feel so bad," she said.

Maude looked at Opal who nodded, "I'm not saying a word. I'm a locked box."

Ruby smiled meekly. A good night's sleep was just what her aching body needed. The Nepali food hadn't been sitting well on her stomach, but she was sure that once she got some sleep, she would wake up feeling refreshed in the morning.

When the three women woke up the next morning, they could hear the streets outside buzzing with life.

"That was the best sleep I ever had," exclaimed Opal. Her hair was sticking out of her messy bun in all directions.

"Speak for yourself," Ruby mumbled. She had been up all night with an upset stomach. After vomiting a few times, she finally fell asleep on the bathroom floor.

"I wondered why it was so easy to sprawl out," Maude said. "Are you feeling better now?"

Ruby nodded and started to brush the tangles out of her long hair.

"What's on the schedule for today?" Opal asked. "Any more monkey temples we can visit?"

"No!" Maude interrupted. "And you ain't bringing a monkey home either."

Opal put on her new Nepali garment she bought from the market yesterday and sulked. "You're always such a killjoy, Maude."

"I say we stay close by the hotel so we don't get lost again," Maude said.

"Fine by me," Ruby agreed.

"Let's go back to the market then. I love this new caftan. I want to get more in some of the other colors," Opal said. She twirled around before rummaging in her bag for the drinks from the market. "Need to get some more of these little babies, too."

"I don't know how you drink that stuff," Maude shivered.

Opal polished off the bottle of rice beer and burped.

"You're such a lady," Ruby said sarcastically.

"At your service," Opal bowed low.

The three women got ready for the day and walked down the stairs to the hotel lobby. Mr. Magar eyed them carefully as they disappeared onto the crowded street just outside of the hotel's door.

"Where to first?" Opal asked.

"What are they doing over there?" Maude asked. She pointed to a group of men and women huddled in a group.

Before Ruby could respond, Opal skipped off to join the crowd.

"We need to get her a leash," Maude whispered to Ruby. They walked over to Opal who was already in the middle of the group.

Opal was sitting on a small cushion on the ground with her hands outstretched. A man was painting her hands in small intricate designs with what looked like mud.

"What in the sam hill are you doing?" Maude asked.

"Mehndi," Opal smiled.

"Do what?" Maude replied.

"Mehndi," Opal said again. "Henna tattoo."

"Oh no, buddy," Maude said. She yanked Opal up from her seat and shook her head. "Ain't no way I'm letting you get a tattoo here."

"Maude, stop it!" Opal said. She sat back down and smiled at the confused group. "Mērō pāgala sāthī." The group laughed and looked over at

Maude. The man smiled and continued to paint Opal's arm.

"What did she just say?" Maude asked Ruby. "Did you hear that?"

Ruby looked just as perplexed as Maude did.

"Opal, when did you learn to, you know, speak like that?" Ruby asked.

Opal rolled her eyes and shook her head. "I speak many languages, Ruby. Always the doubter,"' she smiled. "And it's henna, Maude. It's just a type of paste paint. It won't last forever."

Ruby looked back at Maude who shrugged her shoulders. Opal was always full of surprises.

"You want one of those?" Maude asked Ruby.

"Goodness no," Ruby exclaimed. "I don't want a real tattoo either. They look like they hurt." Ruby rubbed her arm and shuddered.

"I'd love a real one," Opal said. "Maybe we can find one of those around here this afternoon."

"You lie," Maude interjected. "You're afraid of needles."

"I ain't done it!" Opal yelped.

"Y'all quit it," Ruby hissed. The Nepalis were staring between Maude and Opal like spectators at a tennis match.

When Opal's hand and arm hennas were finished, they ventured further into the marketplace. Opal stopped every few feet to try a new food or marvel at a new outfit. The Nepali vendors oohed and aahed over Opal's henna designs. "Take a picture," Opal said proudly.

"I've got to go to the restroom," Maude said to Ruby after a few hours of exploration.

"Me, too," Ruby admitted.

Maude didn't think she could make it back to their hotel in time, so they walked around until they found a vacant restroom up a few stone steps.

"Age before beauty," Opal laughed. She pulled the curtain open for Maude before doubling over in a fit of laughter. "Maude! Your royal throne awaits."

"Oh good God! I ain't gonna do it!" Maude yelled.

"What are y'all going on about?" Ruby asked. She leaned past Maude and peeked into the empty room.

"A hole! A hole in the ground!" Opal howled. She held her stomach and laughed until she couldn't stand up straight.

"Hell no," Maude said. "I'll hold it for the rest of the day if I have to!"

"Come off it, Maude," Ruby said. "It's their custom. I bet you can throw the paper in the hole though."

"Nope," Opal laughed. "They don't have any toilet paper." Opal was near hysterics at this point.

"What do you mean no paper?" Maude asked in a strained voice.

"You have to bring your own," Opal said. "Everyone knows that."

Ruby and Maude stared at Opal with their mouths agape.

"What?" Opal asked. "Y'all just ain't as cultured as me." She pulled the curtain back and hopped down the steps.

"Let's just go back to the hotel," Ruby suggested.

"Good idea," Maude agreed. She hurried down the alleyway back towards the hotel. She had made sure to pay extra attention during their visit to the market. She did not want to end up lost like they were yesterday.

"Is that rain?" Ruby suddenly asked. "Oh no! I think it is!"

A crack of thunder resounded through the marketplace. Ruby shrieked and held onto Opal tightly. The rain began to seep in through the colorful overhangs that hung above the market stalls.

"Hurry!" Maude yelled. "It's coming down like cats and dogs!"

Ruby and Opal hurried quickly behind Maude through the crowd in the sudden downpour. By the time they made it to the front steps of their hotel, they resembled drowned rats. Their clothing and hair stuck to them like glue.

"Let's get up to our room and change clothes. Hopefully this storm will pass over us quickly," Ruby said.

"Hopefully the room ain't flooded this time," Maude laughed. "I'm about to wet myself as it is."

"I mean, no one would be able to tell," Opal shrugged.

Maude shot Opal a dirty look and took the stairs two at a time. She beat Ruby to the bathroom and sighed in relief.

"I don't think it's letting up outside," Opal said. She peered through the light curtains and beckoned Maude over to the window.

"It's a frog strangler for sure," Maude agreed.

"Well, we're supposed to be flying out in the morning," Ruby said as she emerged from the bathroom. "I'm sure it'll be over by then. Fingers crossed for clear skies."

"What are we supposed to do in the meantime?" Opal asked.

"I don't know," Maude said. "We can't go outside, that's for sure."

Opal crossed her arms and pouted on the bed. "I wanted to see more of Nepal. We have to leave in the morning and I didn't get to do what all I wanted to."

"You know Opal, it's almost like you sent us to Nepal on purpose," Maude insinuated.

"I ain't done it!" Opal yelled back. "I just did some research on Nepal after I found those cheap tickets. How was I supposed to know Nepal and Naples weren't the same thing or close by."

"Did the continent of Asia not give it away?" Maude shouted.

"I don't know what the big deal is!" Opal said defiantly. "You've met some amazing people and seen some great sights."

"I signed up for Naples! Not any of these long flights or crazy people!" Maude retorted.

"You sure didn't mind when Reginald was pouring drinks down your throat and rubbing his hands all over you during that long flight," Opal barked.

Ruby had to admit that Opal had a point. The flights were long and they had already encountered so much drama, but they had already had so much fun, too.

"Don't bring up Reginald to me," Maude said. "Ruby's already upset with him."

Ruby snapped her head to look at Maude. "I'm not upset. I just didn't think you were making smart choices where he was concerned."

"You just didn't like the Jameson reference," Maude whispered under her breath.

A pang of regret hit Ruby like a punch to the stomach. She had willed herself not to think about Jameson and she had done a pretty good job thus far.

"Sorry Ruby, that was out of line," Maude said. "You're right, I wasn't being smart. I'm just tired and a little freaked out by all of this. I mean, we've never been away from home and here we are literally across the world."

"I know," Ruby said. "It freaks me out, too."

"I don't know what y'all are talking about," Opal smiled. "We're having the time of our lives!"

The three friends huddled together and watched the rain storm rage outside of the window long into the night. Thanks to Opal, they had plenty of hearty Nepalese food to keep them full.

∞Chapter Eleven∞

The rain did not stop during the night. If anything, it got worse. By the time they got dressed and packed up the next morning, the rain was coming down in sheets so thick they could barely make out the features of the marketplace from their window.

"This weather sure looks bad," Ruby worried, staring out into the torrent.

Maude stood beside her looking just as concerned. "Maybe it'll let up by the time we get to the airport," she said.

They grabbed their bags and carried them down the steps to the hotel lobby.

"Um, how are we supposed to get to the airport in this downpour?" Opal asked.

"No, no, no," Mr. Magar said. He had appeared suddenly behind Opal. "Monsoon, no flights."

"What do you mean no flights?" Maude asked.

"Monsoon," he shrugged. "No flights. The airport is closed."

"How are you supposed to get out of here?" Maude shrieked.

"Not by plane," he continued. "Monsoon season. The rain caused a mudslide and shut down everything flight wise."

"Well this is just great!" Maude snapped. "We'll be stuck here forever."

Mr. Magar gritted his teeth and took a deep breath. "There are other ways. I suggest you take a bus to the border and then take the train."

"The train? There's a train to Italy? No way, no sir!" Maude said. "I ain't getting on a train across multiple continents."

Mr. Magar waited for her to finish. "A bus or a car to the train station. A train to New Delhi. Then you catch flight from there."

"Oh," Maude replied. "I guess that's not so bad. India is right next door on the map, so no big deal. How do we get a car to the train?"

"I can make some calls for you," Mr. Magar said. He disappeared behind the counter and picked up the phone. He was ready to get these three on their way. There was no telling how much the plumbing issues would cost to fix. These women were nice enough, but they were costing him money each day that they stayed. Against his better judgment, he promised Kamal he would take care of these tourists and make sure they had a nice layover here in Nepal. His nephew was pretty enamored with the small crazy one who was currently dancing around the lobby by herself.

"At least our feet will be closer to the ground on a train," Maude said. "We don't have the best record in the air."

"I bet a train ride through the countryside would be beautiful!" Ruby exclaimed. "Opal! Come here."

Opal floated her way over to her. "You rang?" she smiled.

"Mr. Magar said he's going to get us some train tickets to India. I guess the airport there is fine," Ruby explained.

"Ohhh, a train ride. Just tell me when!" Opal replied.

They sat down on the stiff couch in the lobby waiting for Mr. Magar to finish his call. He hung up the phone and smiled. He waved the three girls over to the counter and began writing notes down on a pad of paper.

"The train leaves after lunch. It is about a three hour drive to the station. I will have someone take you," he said.

"Oh! That's very nice of you, sir," Ruby smiled.

"Three hours?" Maude huffed.

"Anything for Kamal's friends," he replied hastily . "I'll have the car brought around."

"Kamal's uncle is so sweet. Good looks must run in the family," Opal smiled.

"What in the devil did you say to that boy?" Maude whispered to Opal.

Opal batted her eyes and smiled. "What can I say? I'm a delight." She winked at Maude and then smiled at Maude's dumbfounded look. "Don't worry about it," she winked again. "Let's go!" She gathered her bags and large pillow and followed Mr. Magar to the door.

"Don't we have to pay?" Ruby asked.

"Shh, Ruby. Just go with it," Maude whispered.

Ruby shrugged her shoulders at Maude's comment, but the idea of leaving this beautiful hotel without paying wasn't sitting right with her. She leaned over and whispered to one of the young bellboys who had helped her before, "Just out of curiosity, how much does a room in this hotel normally go for?"

He thought earnestly for a moment. "I don't know, but I heard they cost over a thousand rupees a night!" he said in amazement.

"Oh dear," Ruby shuddered. Maybe skipping out was the only way they could afford to leave the country.

"How much would that be in American dollars?" she asked nervously.

"American dollars?" he exclaimed. "I have never seen American dollars. But around ten American dollars."

Ruby was stunned. "Ten dollars?" she asked.

"Oh yes ma'am," he nodded.

Ruby smiled. She opened her bag and took a dollar bill out and handed it to the young man.

Tears welled up in his eyes. "Oh no, ma'am. I can't take this."

"I insist," she said.

He thanked her profusely, almost tripping over a chair as he turned to walk away. Ruby smiled to herself. It was amazing that such a little thing could make someone so happy. She waited until Mr. Magar's back was turned, then she slipped three ten dollar bills beside the drawer where he kept his till, directly underneath the pad of paper he had been taking notes on. He had been so nice about everything. He deserved a little tip.

Ruby gathered up her things. Her head was starting to hurt and she was more than ready to get on the train and hopefully take a nap. She wasn't sure how long the trip would take, but Maude had assured her that India was directly across the border, so it couldn't be far. They loaded their bags in the car underneath the hotel overhang. Ruby and Maude slid into the back seat once Opal claimed the front passenger seat as hers. Neither Ruby nor Maude argued with her.

Mr. Magar's driver got in the driver's seat and before they pulled onto the main street, Kamal's rickshaw pulled up beside them. He waved to Opal with a sorrowful look on his face. Opal jumped out of the car and wrapped her arms around Kamal. She planted a big kiss on his lips and Kamal's cheeks flushed vibrantly.

"If you're ever in the States, give me a ring!" she said. She climbed back into the car and blew him a kiss behind the glass window. Maude and

Ruby's eyes were larger than saucers, but they held their tongue.

Once they got onto the road and lost in traffic, Maude leaned over the seat and whispered, "Damn Opal."

"What can I say. I like them tall, dark, and handsome," she giggled.

"You're a mess, you know that, right?" Maude laughed under her breath.

Opal shrugged and watched the rain pool along the roadside. No wonder the airport had closed down, the runways couldn't handle this much rain.

The bumpy road had jostled Opal to sleep not long after they left the hotel. Ruby and Maude took turns napping and asking the driver how much longer the trip would be. The driver parked them directly in front of the station entrance and helped them unload their belongings once they arrived. "Give the attendant Mr. Magar's name and he will take care of you. Goodbye! Rat Pack forever!"

He sped off before they could return the goodbye. He was exhausted from the three hour trip.

"I don't even want to know," Ruby said. She held her hand up so Maude and Opal wouldn't say anything. "Come on, let's get out of this rain."

They quickly hurried into the station and looked around for the front desk. Maude found it first and dropped the bags in front of the counter. "Mr. Magar from Kathmandu sent us here for train tickets."

"Ah, yes," the attendant replied. "I have them right here."

The tall man helped them carry their bags to a passenger train car waiting on the tracks. He slid the larger luggage into the slots above the seats on the right wall and instructed them to store their smaller bags underneath the bunk beds on the left wall. The bunk beds were three beds stacked atop each other.

"Why do we need beds?" Maude asked. "It took us three hours to get here. Aren't we nearly there yet?"

"It's a twenty-five hour ride via the train to New Delhi, ma'am," he said. "Trust me when I say you want the sleeper car."

"I'm sorry, what?" Maude asked.

"Twenty-five hours and you have a private sleeper car courtesy of Mr. Magar. I'm confused," he replied.

"Twenty-five hours?" Maude repeated. "No. No way in the name of Jesus am I riding on this steel death trap for twenty-five hours. Nope. Never in a million years."

Opal climbed up to the highest bunk and stretched her arms and legs out. "This is great!"

"Let's make the best of it, Maude. Which bunk do you want?" Ruby asked. She was always trying to make the best of every situation.

Maude glared at her and sat down in one of the seats. She crossed her arms and looked out the window that was blurred from the constant downpour.

"Ok, I take that as you want the bottom bunk. I'll take the middle one and we'll hope Opal doesn't fall off the top," Ruby smiled. She certainly didn't want to ride in a small and cramped passenger car for twenty-five hours, but she didn't see any other way to get to Naples. "Let's just make the best of it."

Maude flung herself across the seat and said, "I just want to be at the beach."

"And we're getting there," Opal smiled down from the top bunk. "We just have to take some detours first."

"We've had a lot of detours, Opal," Maude snapped.

"You complain too much," Opal replied. "You're getting to travel the world. Most people like us don't get to do that, Maude. I'm thankful for this trip. There's not anyone I'd rather be on a cross country trip with besides you two."

Ruby smiled and even Maude gave a sideways grin.

"I guess we'll just have to make the best of it," Maude said. Her mood shifted considerably after Opal's pep talk. "It's lunchtime. Where are the eats?"

"Sounds like a job for me!" Opal said. She leapt down from the top bunk and landed gracefully on her feet. She took off and Ruby settled down next to Maude.

"It's been an adventure for sure," Ruby smiled. She pressed her face against the glass and tried to look through the rain for a last good look at Nepal.

"I just wish I could lose this headache. It's got to be the food or the altitude or something."

"Yea. My stomach hasn't been the same lately either. Speaking of which, there's a bathroom on this thing, right?" Maude said.

The train was starting to leave the station. Opal reappeared with good news. "There's so much food on board. I didn't see very many people though. Guess that's more food for us!"

Maude perked up at the good news. Maybe this wouldn't be such a bad train ride after all.

"So, I gotta know Opal, what exactly happened with you and Kamal?" Maude asked.

"I'm a lady," Opal smiled. "A lady never kisses and tells."

"You ain't done it!" Maude laughed. She hurled a pillow at Opal who had already climbed back up to the top bunk.

"Which one of us is a lady?" Ruby laughed.

"Not me, that's for dang sure," Maude said. She stretched her arms to the ceiling and stood up carefully. She walked to the door and opened it. At least with the narrow hallways, Opal was less likely to get lost.

The train was gathering speed and they watched the rain drops rush off the glass. "Guess there's no turning back now," Ruby said. She had to stop watching the fast paced changing scenery because it was making her dizzy.

"Does this train make any stops?" Maude asked.

"Yes, but we don't get off until we hear them say New Delhi," Opal explained.

Maude rolled her eyes and wished she had another pillow to throw at Opal. This was going to be a long trip after all.

～Chapter Twelve～

As the afternoon wore on, Ruby took out the postcards she had bought in Nepal, Germany, and New York City. The images on the front were beautiful, but somehow they couldn't do justice to all the sights and sounds of the places she had experienced. She chose one with a picture of a temple from Nepal and bit her pen for a few moments before she began to write the note to her parents. How could she begin to describe everything that had happened in such a short period of time?

> *Hi Mom and Dad,*
> *As you can see from the front, we've had a slight detour on our way to Italy. We're ok! It's been a wonderful adventure so far and I'm*

*honestly having the time of my life! I'll tell you
all about it when I get home. Opal and Maude
are the best when they're not trying to kill each
other! They are keeping me in stitches.*

*I love you both! Tell Robert and Tammy I
said hello!*

Love, Ruby

She sorted through the cards and found the
perfect one for Jameson. Before she even realized
what she was doing, she had started scribbling a
hasty note to him about her trip thus far. It seemed
like the most natural thing in the world to do.

Jameson,

*You will never believe the things we've
done so far on this trip! Opal sent us halfway
around the world. I'm sure you're not
completely surprised. You've always said she
could get lost in a flour sack. She will never
change....*

Ruby stopped writing mid sentence and stared
at the card before her. Jameson was the first one she
always talked to about everything. He was the one
she had hoped to grow old with. He had always
been the champion in her corner. Now, all that was
gone. He had seen to that before she left. He
wanted to find himself and see where things went.
Meanwhile she was supposed to wait and see if she
fit anywhere in his future plans.

Who was she kidding? Jameson was the catch
of the county. He had girls lining up for his
affections. Ruby knew he would never cheat on

her, but maybe now that they were on a pause as Jameson called it, he would find someone else. Maybe he was bored with Ruby and needed some excitement in his life.

She looked down at the postcard again. Jameson had been the one she could always turn to. A few weeks ago, he would have loved to have heard about this trip. Now he was a closed chapter of her life. No matter how badly she wanted it, he wasn't coming back and she couldn't expect it to happen. She took the postcard and ripped it up. Ruby wasn't going to waste another minute wishing he would come back. At least, she would do her very best not to waste anymore time on him.

Her thoughts were interrupted by Opal's snoring and Maude's mouth breathing. She wasn't sure how they could both fall asleep so easily in the most random places. She knew they were tired because she was tired, too, but her mind was too busy racing. The time zones were affecting her ability to sleep and focus on anything other than the present. Maybe she would finally be able to rest once they got to Italy. The constant back and forth and uncertainties of planes, trains, and rickshaws were becoming a little too much. At least they finally had a viable plan of action. Once they arrived at the train station in New Delhi, they would take a bus to the airport and fly to Italy. She could practically feel the warm salty air on her skin as she closed her eyes. Just a few more hours on this train. She was asleep before she could put away her writings.

Maude was the first one to wake when the dinner bell rang. She poked Opal and Ruby awake and they sleepily followed her down the narrow hallway between the cars. They found the dining car and sat down at a rickety table that swayed slightly with each bump along the railway. Much to Maude's delight, they had a functioning bar on board.

"Well, I know where I'll be spending my evening," Maude laughed.

"I think I'm going to give up alcohol," Opal said.

Maude and Ruby looked at her like she had two heads. "Why?" Maude asked.

"That rice beer didn't sit well with me," Opal explained.

"That's because you drank three bottles one right after the other and they were hot. They'd been in your bag all day," Maude replied.

"That's why I'm giving it up," Opal shrugged. "I'll discover it again once we get to Italy. Italian wine is good for the heart."

Maude rolled her eyes and shook her head. Opal was a nutcase through and through.

"I'm with Opal on this one," Ruby laughed. "My stomach is all over the place. I don't want to chance anything."

"More for me then!" Maude lauded.

More people began to pile into the dining cart one by one. Soon the entire car was full and there was not an empty seat in sight.

"So much for not many people," Maude said under her breath.

"I guess they all boarded during the stops," Opal replied. She shrugged her shoulders and waved at anyone who would look her way. "I hope they bring us some of that golden bread. I can't stop thinking about it."

Ruby nodded. The bread had been really good and had not upset her stomach. Maybe she should stick to bland foods like bread and pasta once they got to Italy. Her Rhinestone stomach was not used to the spicy food that Nepal had to offer. She would rather be sick than seen as rude, so she usually ate what was put in front of her. She did not want to offend anyone or stick out like a common tourist. It appeared that Opal could and would eat just about anything, but that was not the case with Maude. Maude was as finicky as they came. If it wasn't chicken, she probably wouldn't eat it. On this trip already there had been some close calls where Opal promised Maude the meat was chicken. She admitted to Ruby later that she wasn't certain what it was, but it hadn't killed anyone yet.

Dinner was uneventful. Maude filled up on beer and bread. Thankfully they had a salad that Ruby was able to eat without feeling the rush of nausea rise in her throat. Opal ate the entire four course meal, even though no one was able to explain what exactly it was. Opal was like a steel trap when it came to food.

They walked back to their sleeper car in near darkness. It was pitch black outside and the car did not offer many lighting opportunities. Opal climbed up to her top bunk and was sound asleep before Maude exited the bathroom. Ruby climbed into the middle bunk and listened to the rhythm of the wheels against the tracks. Several people were chatting loudly outside the door. For a moment, Ruby thought they were in a heated argument, but when the laughter broke out, she breathed a sigh of relief. She listened as they moved down the corridor before falling asleep.

Opal was the first one awake the next morning. She was fully rested now and ready for the next adventure. She hopped off her bunk and unlatched the belt that held her suitcase together. Most of her clothes fell out on the floor.

"What in the world are you trying to do, wake the dead?" Maude grumbled.

"I'm trying to clean up the mess you made with my suitcase," Opal retorted. She refolded her clothes and the suitcase was actually beginning to look neat and organized.

Ruby had almost forgotten that she and Maude had packed all Opal's things before they left.

"You're lucky we did. You would've been nekked by now if we hadn't," Maude said, yawning loudly.

"Ooooh, that's a great idea! Maybe we can visit one of those nude beaches while we're in Italy," Opal said, clapping her hands together.

"We are not going to a nude beach!" Maude replied, lifting her head up quickly and hitting it on Ruby's bunk. "Ow!"

"Serves you right for raining on my parade. Ruby'll go with me; won't you Ruby?" Opal pleaded with her other friend.

"I'm not going to a nude beach, Opal." Ruby said, sitting up carefully to avoid the bunk above her.

"Y'all are just no fun!" Opal lamented.

Maude rubbed her head and rolled out of bed. "There ain't nothing rude about it. We ain't gallivanting around Europe nekkid!"

"It's not all over Europe. It's just Italy," Opal explained.

"I don't care which part of Europe it is. We ain't doing it!" Maude huffed.

"We'll see," Opal smirked under her breath.

"Can we change the subject?" Ruby asked.

"Yeah, let's talk about something important. When's breakfast?" Maude asked.

"You keep eating like that and you're going to be too fat for our trip to the nude beach," Opal said.

"We ain't going to a nude beach!" Maude shouted.

Opal opened her mouth to respond, but Ruby spoke up instead. "I think breakfast is a good idea. Maybe the dining car is open."

Opal and Maude followed Ruby towards the dining car. They found three empty seats in the corner. The car seemed to be moving from side to side more than it was yesterday. They looked out the window as grayness washed over the train.

"What in the world?" Ruby asked.

"It's a sandstorm, ma'am," the waiter explained.

"That's a lot of dirt," Maude said.

"We have dirt like that back home," Opal assured the waiter.

The waiter ignored Opal and set a plate of flatbread and crepes before them. There were also several dips and chutneys in small bowls. Opal grabbed the bowl of spiced potatoes and smelled them.

"Ahh, nothing like a good potato! Here Maude, try some," she ordered. She dumped some on Maude's plate. Maude looked miffed and pushed the potatoes around with her small fork.

"I don't want those!" she huffed. "Too much pepper! Take them back!"

"One of these days you'll learn to appreciate fine cuisine like us, Maude," Opal sighed.

Ruby let Opal dish out potatoes on her plate. She even enjoyed the flatbread and lentil crepes.

Maude stuffed her face with the flatbread and spit out the bite of lentil crepe. Ruby shot her a look and smiled sheepishly at the passing waiter. He looked like he was about done with them already. Ruby waited for Opal to finish eating before she piled the dishes and napkins into the center of the table. Maude stood up shakily and leaned on Opal for stability.

"Is it just me or this train feeling a little wonky?" Maude asked.

"Just you, I'm afraid," Opal smiled. She grabbed Maude by the shoulders and attempted to guide her back to their car. Ruby had the sneaking suspicion that Opal was guiding Maude into the walls and other passengers on purpose.

They returned to their cabin and packed up their bags. The train was definitely rocking worse than it was the day before. Maude sat down and held her head. She tried to watch Opal packing, but Opal's dancing was adding to her motion sickness. By the look on Ruby's face, she, too, was feeling a little woozy.

"We definitely need to wear our Nepal shirts so that we can find each other in the crowds," Ruby announced.

"Find each other where? We're just getting off the train and finding a taxi," Maude said, holding her hand to her mouth.

Ruby looked at her. "Maude, we've almost lost each other at every stop."

"Yeah, Maude, you lag behind something terrible," Opal agreed.

Maude glared at her, but obliged by putting on her shirt as directed.

"This time try to keep up," Opal added.

Maude was a little worse for the wear by the time the train made it into the station. The terminal was overrun with people pushing and shoving this way and that. Maude was jostled between two families trying to get on the train she was exiting. She looked up hoping to catch a glimpse of Ruby or Opal, but they were buried in a sea of sarees and turbans.

"There's a thousand people wearing white shirts!" Maude commented to herself. "I'll never find them in this mess. Opal!" Maude yelled Opal's name twice more before Opal popped up beside her.

"I told you to hurry up. Ruby is getting the tickets for the bus," Opal smiled.

"What bus?" Maude asked. She continued to be pushed from side to side.

"The bus to the airport," Opal explained. "We can't expect you to walk in your condition, remember?"

"I swear to God, Opal, one of these days I will kill you," Maude growled.

"Well, as long as it ain't today!" Opal said cheerfully. "Now come on!"

∽Chapter Thirteen∽

"I don't know about this!" Maude yelled. Her knuckles were white as she tightly gripped the seat in front of her.

"This is great!" Opal cheered.

Ruby had curled up in the fetal position on the floor of the bus in front of Opal and Maude. "Tell me when it's over," she wailed.

"Do they let just anyone drive?" Maude yelled. "This is insane!"

Maude and Ruby seemed to be the only passengers who felt uneasy about the ride. Every other passenger stayed in their seat or stood and held onto the cable running the length of the bus.

"Slow down!" Maude yelled to no one in particular. Her constant yells and moans were garnering the attention of the other passengers who shot her dirty looks and spoke in hushed whispers to each other.

The driver took a particularly sharp curve for which Maude was not prepared. She flew forward and landed in the lap of an older gentleman. He smiled up at her, laughing with a gaping hole where his front tooth should have been. His wife was less amused and began speaking rapidly in Hindi. Maude got up quickly, tried to regain her footing, and apologized to everyone around. "Sorry!"

The woman glared at her for a few seconds, then she turned to her husband and expressed her displeasure at his happiness.

'How much longer?" Ruby moaned.

"I don't know what the big fuss is!" Opal said as they went over a pothole in the road. "It's not that bad."

"Speak for yourself!" Ruby hissed. She was being jostled around like a beach ball on a wave in the ocean.

"Where did he even learn to drive!" Maude shouted. "This is insane!"

Maude was clearly making the other passengers uncomfortable. She was causing a scene, but she did not seem to care. "Insane! Do you hear me? Insane!" she bellowed.

Opal shook her head and looked solemn. "You're embarrassing me in front of my new friends," she said. She stood up and walked to the front of the bus, stumbling the whole way there.

"Friends?" Maude yelled after her. "You don't know these people!"

Opal melted into the crowd at the front of the bus and Maude lost sight of her. She reached at her feet and yanked Ruby's arm. "Get up here!" she snarled.

"Where'd Opal go?" Ruby wondered.

"Hell if I know!" Maude grumbled.

Laughter permeated through the crowd and everyone turned to look at Maude and Ruby near the back of the bus. "What?" Maude asked grumpily.

The crowd laughed even harder and Maude could finally see why. Opal had pulled herself up on the cable and was entertaining her supposed new friends with her antics.

The bus skidded to a halt to make way for a convoy of cows crossing the road ahead. Opal continued to swing on the cable and entertain everyone, except for Maude and Ruby.

"We can't take her anywhere. You know that, right?" Ruby asked Maude.

"Oh dear God in heaven! What is she doing now?" Maude asked. She looked up to see Opal dancing with two of the young men standing with her at the front of the bus.

Ruby and Maude watched as the three of them danced for a few minutes until one of them pulled out a pipe and offered it to Opal.

"Oh my God! What is she doing? Opal no!" Maude yelled at her.

"Opal put that down!" Ruby yelled.

But Opal wasn't listening. She smiled and inhaled deeply. By the time Maude and Ruby had staggered their way to the front of the bus, Opal had inhaled deeply a few more times from the swirling smoke of the pipe.

"Opal, what are you doing?" Maude demanded.

"It's an Indian peace pipe," Opal smiled, a bit more calmly than she normally did.

"That ain't a damn peace pipe, you idiot!" Maude yelled.

"Maude," Opal looked over at her, "these are my friends. They offered me the pipe of friendship. It would be rude not to take it."

"Opal! Put that down!" Ruby told her.

Opal smiled. "You two wouldn't understand," she said dismissively. "Americans, am I right?" Opal laughed with her new friends.

"You have lost your mind!" Maude rolled her eyes and snatched the pope from Opal's hands and thrust it back to the two young men who smiled at the scene before them. Ruby helped Opal back to their seats at the back of the bus.

"Are we there yet? This is ridiculous! Now we've got to manage Opal who's high as a damn kite!" Maude howled. "Don't look at me like that!" Maude had reached her limit with her fellow passengers, Opal, and life in general.

"I think I see the airport ahead," Ruby declared.

"Well it's about damn time!" Maude scowled. She crossed her arms and kicked the suitcase near her.

"Ok, we're here. Let's get our things and oh God!" Ruby squealed.

Opal had already descended from the bus and was dancing in the street with some street musicians outside of the airport. She was heavily intoxicated on whatever was in that pipe and she looked lost in her own world. She had a big goofy smile plastered across her face.

"Get the bags, Maude, and I'll get Opal," Ruby sighed. She left Maude struggling to unload the bags from underneath the seats and from the surrounding aisles. She grabbed Opal by the shoulders and shook her vigorously.

"Opal! Snap out of it! We've got a plane to catch!" Ruby yelled. Opal was in a whole other world thanks to her experience with the friendship pipe.

"Feel the beat, Rubes! I can feel it! Boohoo yea!" Opal sang and swayed along to the beat of the stringed instruments. She shimmied and shook her way down to the ground where she then started to inch her way across the road like an inchworm.

"Opal, I swear to everything that is holy, get off the ground and come on!" Ruby stomped her foot and demanded that Opal stand up. She kicked at Opal's outstretched feet and decided the best course of action would be to scoop Opal up and carry her inside by herself.

It proved to be more difficult a feat than Ruby anticipated. She had to flag down a man with a cart to assist her because, although Opal was thin and small framed, she was fast and hyped up. The man threw Opal over his shoulder and stomped towards the entrance of the airport. Ruby found

Maude and helped her carry the bags and pillows to the check in desk where they found Opal on the floor.

"She poke me!" the man howled. He was holding one hand over his left eye and pointed his other hand at Opal who was smiling up at him. "She crazy!" He stormed off leaving a very perplexed Maude and Ruby to deal with Opal.

"I'll see about getting us tickets," Ruby said. She had already had the pleasure of dealing with an intoxicated Opal and decided it was Maude's turn. Before Maude could object, Ruby hurried off to the row of counters.

"Get up fruit cake," Maude ordered. Opal continued to make snow angels on the floor. Travelers had to step over her to avoid tripping. Maude did her best to smile at the passersby, but Opal's writhing was getting even more out of hand.

"Okay, I got the tickets," Ruby returned, waving the three pieces of paper in her hand. She looked down at Opal, then back to see the aggravated look on Maude's face.

"We're in luck. There's a flight leaving within the hour headed to Istanbul," Ruby explained to Maude.

"Istanbul? We're trying to get to Italy, not Istanbul," Maude frowned.

"Apparently, we have to catch a flight from there to Italy. This was all they had," Ruby said. "At least we're getting closer."

Maude grunted. "At least I can get rid of the bags now," she nuffed. She tossed the suitcases on the belt and turned to find Opal.

"Wheeeeeeeee," Opal was up and dancing once again. Apparently she could hear the music in her head when no one else could. Maude and Ruby had never seen an official belly dance before, but they were sure that Opal's version wasn't an accurate rendition.

"Well, at least we're getting closer," Maude mumbled. "Where is the terminal?"

Ruby looked around. "Um, this way looks right," she decided.

Maude grabbed the growing number of bags and Ruby took Opal's hand like a small child. Opal mistook the gesture and began an animated rumba with Ruby who was mortified by the attention they were getting.

"I'm going to have to kill," Maude mumbled to herself. "It's the only way. I'm going to have to kill her and drag her body to Italy."

Ruby managed to pull away from Opal's embrace just in time to see the gift shop. "Oh look, we have to stop for just a second," she squealed.

"We don't have time," Maude told her through gritted teeth.

"Just a second. We need to get souvenirs from our time in India," Ruby explained.

Maude rolled her eyes and dropped the bags while Ruby went inside. Maude knew there was no use fighting with her. Ruby never saw a gift shop she didn't like. She turned in time to see Opal once again trying to dance with a strange man. He was not as smitten with her antics as the men on the bus. Maude barely got Opal away before he caused a commotion.

"Good Lord, Opal. You're going to get us thrown in jail in the middle of India!" Maude reprimanded.

"India? Like Indian. I'm part Indian," Opal raised one hand to her mouth and began an exaggerated chant and stomped the ground in a circle with her other hand in the air.

Maude wanted to melt into the ground. Things got even worse when Opal began to dance around in a circle and waved her arms up and down and side to side.

"Stop that right now!" Maude demanded.

Ruby emerged from the gift shop to a full spectacle. Opal was fully into her American Indian tribal dance, but stopped when she saw Ruby walking towards her. She held up her hand and said, "How, pale face. I come in peace."

"We're all pale white, you nimwit. Now come on!" Maude told her.

"Me no go. Me stay here on sacred land," Opal spoke like a bad actor in a wild west movie. Maude had never been so embarrassed in her entire life.

"Opal, we've got to go or we'll miss our plane," Ruby urged her.

"Me no go," Opal said firmly.

Maude's patience was wearing thin. She took the hardcover tourist book that Ruby had just bought and popped Opal in the head. She hit her harder than she intended, but it seemed to do the trick. Opal shook her head several times, but followed Ruby without any further dance recitals. Ruby looked over at Maude who merely shrugged and picked the bags back up.

After three wrong turns, they finally found the correct terminal for their flight without another minute to spare. Once they reached the line to board the plane, Opal had slumped over onto Ruby's shoulder. Ruby helped her walk and looked around for Maude to help, but Maude was still struggling with the pillows, travel bags, and new souvenirs. The attendant stopped them once they got to the front of the line and asked if Opal was ok.

"Just ignore her," Ruby smiled and patted Opal. "Too much alcohol." Ruby smiled again and hoped it was enough to get past the attendant checking the tickets. The man looked confused, but let them pass nevertheless.

"We're riding in that?" Maude looked at the plane.

"Looks that way," Ruby replied.

Maude looked concerned. "Looks a little worse for the wear."

"It'll be fine," Ruby assured her. "Now help me with Opal!".

Maude helped her dump Opal into the first seat they found and buckled her in safely.

"I'm not sitting with her," Maude said. "It's your turn. I'm sitting as far away as possible."

A man in the seat next to Opal got up and moved so Ruby could sit near her friend who had already slumped over in the seat. Ruby glared at Maude who pranced down the aisle seven rows back.

"How long is this flight?" Ruby politely asked the attendant at the front of the plane.

"About nine hours, madam," the stewardess replied.

Nine hours. Maude wasn't going to like that. Suddenly, Ruby was glad she was sitting with Opal and not Maude.

❦ Chapter Fourteen ❦

Nine hours on yet another flight did not sound fun to Ruby either, but she was ready to land in Italy. Once they landed in Istanbul, one more small flight would get them to Rome. She did not even care what the weather would be like once they landed in Italy, as long as their feet landed on Italian soil. Opal had fallen asleep, or maybe she had fallen into a coma from the effects of the drugs and Maude's attack. Either way, she was softly snoring and looked peaceful. Ruby took her shoes off and decided it would be best to land in Italy feeling well rested. Hopefully the noise of the plane would settle the further they ascended.

"What kind of crazy contraption is this?" Maude asked no one in particular.

The gentleman beside her leaned over close and explained to her in a raised voice that they were riding in a DC6. He described it as one of the finest turboprops in the air today. "Very nice," he said. "Very nice."

Maude did not share his enthusiasm for the plane. It was twice as loud at the jet they'd flown on earlier and three times as bouncy. She swore her innards were going to be jarred loose. She grabbed for the armrest when they hit an especially turbulent patch of air.

"Oh my God! We're going to die!" Maude yelled. The man beside her patted her arm kindly, but it did little to comfort her. Ruby awoke violently and stretched to look at Maude a few rows behind her. Thankfully Opal was still sawing logs next to her. The turbulence and engine noise did not seem to faze her one bit.

Maude patted her chest several times before she couldn't stand it any longer. She jumped up and ran for the restroom at the back of the plane. Thankfully, there were not any other passengers waiting in line. She emerged from the restroom looking rather green a few minutes later. By the time she got halfway up the aisle, they hit another pocket of air and she tumbled forward. When she managed to get to her feet, she turned and headed for the bathroom again.

Ruby was worried about Maude. She did not seem to travel well. Maybe Opal should have offered her that pipe. On second thought, Ruby was glad she hadn't, because there was no way she could manage the two of them high as kites. This had certainly been an adventure already. She wasn't sure what else could go wrong on this adventure. She could just imagine Jameson's face when he heard about it. Ruby stopped for a moment at the thought. Best not to think about him and the way his eyes danced when he laughed. She needed to shake the thoughts of him out of her head for good. The constant shaking of the plane was helping with that. She wondered if she should wake up Opal, but she decided to leave her be. Her snores were barely audible over the noise anyway.

Maude staggered back to her seat and fastened her seatbelt. She groaned loudly. The man beside her handed her a cup of tea.

"What is this?" Maude asked.

"For the stomach," he told her gently.

Maude was beyond caring. She downed the drink in one large gulp, burning the back of her throat slightly in the process. Whether it actually settled her stomach or not, she didn't know. The next thing Maude knew, the stewardess was waking her up and asking her to lift her seat forward. They were about to land. The old man smiled at Maude who nodded groggily. She noticed Ruby wide awake near the front of the plane. Opal was still fast asleep. Maybe Maude did hit her too hard. Too late to take that moment back though. She could always apologize for it later on.

Once the plane landed, Maude had to wait for the rows in front of her to leave before she could. She couldn't help Ruby drag Opal off the plane. She was once again stuck with the bags anyway. By the time she got off the plane herself, she had lost Ruby and Opal in the crowd again.

Maude had a hard time finding Ruby and Opal after they exited the plane. Opal was much less animated, but she seemed to be getting her second wind. Ruby looked paler than normal, but smiled broadly when Maude walked up to them.

"Are you feeling okay?" Maude asked Ruby.

"The flight got to my stomach just a bit," Ruby told her.

"Yeah, mine too," Maude admitted. "How are you feeling Opal?"

"I had the strangest dream. I can't seem to shake it," Opal said seriously.

"What did you dream about?" Ruby asked.

"It's impossible really. I was minding my own business and Maude hit me upside the head. My head hurt, it still does. It's the strangest thing. I mean, I know Maude has a bad temper and all, but even she wouldn't be that dumb. It's weird," Opal rubbed her head. "I think I even have a bruise."

Maude gritted her teeth and silently took back any apology she had been on the verge of saying.

"You're probably just tired," Ruby assured her. She shook her head at Maude and silently begged her not to haul off and hit Opal again. "We should check on our next flight," Ruby quickly changed the subject.

"Like I said, strange," Opal shrugged.

"Let's go on then," Ruby smiled.

"Yeah, I eventually want to get to Italy," Maude told them.

Opal continued to rub her head as she followed Ruby up to the counter for the tickets. Maude stayed close to the bags and counted to one hundred with her eyes closed.

"What time is our next flight?" Maude asked when Opal and Ruby had rejoined her.

"At eight," Ruby said.

"What time is it now?" Maude looked down at her watch which was still set on Rhinestone time. That wouldn't do her any good. "I don't even know what day it is."

"Me either," Ruby admitted.

"Where are we exactly?" Opal asked, looking around.

"Istanbul, Turkey," Ruby replied.

"Hmm, I don't like turkey. I prefer ham," Opal said.

Maude rolled her eyes and sighed audibly. "Count to one hundred, or two hundred better yet," Ruby whispered to her.

They looked around and finally saw a clock on the wall above the arrivals gate.

"Looks like it's 5:30," Ruby said.

"In the morning or night?" Opal asked.

"It's the evening, Opal," Ruby explained.

"So we have two and a half hours before the next flight. Let's find something to eat. But nothing too rich. I'm still a little queasy," Maude suggested.

"Yea, I'm famished," Opal agreed. "But no turkey, ok?"

"Oh good grief!" Maude mumbled.

They found a kebab stand and managed to clear off a table in the corner.

"What kind of meat is this?" Maude asked.

"Chicken," Opal said a little too quickly.

Ruby looked down quickly to avoid Maude's eye. She knew good and well it probably wasn't chicken, although she had no idea what it actually was.

Maude smelled it and nervously took a bite. It wasn't chicken. It might have been beef. She wasn't exactly sure what it was, but she had to admit that it wasn't half bad. She decided to believe it was beef and eat it without giving it another thought.

Ruby only finished half of hers. She said her stomach was just too unsettled to handle any more of the skewer. Opal ate the last half of Ruby's kebab after finishing her own. She threw the trash away and asked where they wanted to go next.

"I'd like to find a gift shop," Ruby said cheerfully. "Time for another shirt, Maude!"

"There's the surprise of the century," Maude smiled.

"Mary had a little lamb, little lamb, little lamb. Mary had a little lamb, but we ate it whole," Opal sang.

"Shut up, Opal!" Maude demanded. She could feel her stomach do a little flip.

"Well, we did. And you liked it," Opal sneered. She considered herself a wizard at changing Maude's bland culinary palette.

"It was beef!" Maude said. "Right?"

"Whatever helps you sleep at night. Baa baa black sheep," Opal sang again.

Maude set their bags down outside the shop and left Opal to guard their things.

"Baby sheep, you're good to eat," Opal sang.

Maude plugged her fingers in her ear and followed Ruby into the cramped and dark gift shop to get away from Opal. She was immediately overwhelmed by the smell of incense. She held her nose and motioned for Ruby to hurry up. Ruby had never hurried a day in her life when it came to shopping, so Maude knew it was a lost cause and rejoined Opal outside of the shop.

"So help me God, Opal, if you sing one more note!" Maude said.

"I know, I know, you're going to kill me," Opal smiled. She knew Maude would never actually kill her, at least she didn't think she would. Everyone had their snapping point. Best not to tempt her anymore than she already had.

"What's Ruby buying this time?" Opal asked.

"God knows!" Maude said. She rolled her eyes at the thought of yet another shirt for them all to match in.

To pass the time, Opal waved at every passerby and smiled genuinely. She found it interesting that almost every single person who met her eyes smiled back. There was the occasional grumpy passerby, but most everyone genuinely softened and returned her smile. Even Maude noticed and began to interact.

As predicted, Ruby emerged a few minutes later with three matching shirts, packets of teas, bags of spices, and a leather bag emblazoned with a black cat silhouette.

"A cat bag? You bought a cat bag?" Maude asked.

"The gentleman in there has the sweetest kitty I've ever seen! He let me pet it and everything!" Ruby exclaimed.

That was all Opal needed to hear. She was on her feet in no time and bounded into the shop. A few minutes later she came out of the shop with an identical bag.

"Are you kidding me!" Maude exclaimed.

"Did you want one, too?" Ruby asked.

"No!" Maude retorted. "I don't want a cat bag! I hate cats!"

"How could you hate cats?" Opal gasped. "I won't stand for it!" She grasped Maude by the shoulders and marched her into the shop to pet the gorgeous fluffy cat that she and Ruby were already so smitten with.

Ruby could hear them arguing within moments of stepping foot inside. She giggled when she heard Maude say in no uncertain terms that Opal could not buy an actual kitten and take it home. A very unhappy Opal emerged from the shop pouting a few minutes later.

"I guess I'll find something else to put in my cat bag," she huffed.

"Come on, enough of that," directed Maude. "We have a flight to catch."

The three women gathered their bags, pillows, and souvenirs and made their way across the airport to board their final flight to Rome. They were all more than ready to finally begin their dream vacation in Italy. It had been one adventure after another getting to this final leg. Maybe one day they could laugh about it.

"Hurry up, Ruby," Maude called over her shoulder. "I'm ready to get this over with."

Ruby quickened her pace to catch up with Maude who was practically running to the airplane.

"One more flight. Just a few more hours and I'll be in Italy," Maude said. She was suddenly giddy at the thought.

Maude stopped short when she saw the plane they were riding in. It was smaller than the one they'd just arrived in.

"That thing's only got two engines. The last one had four," Maude told Ruby.

"It'll be fine, Maude. This isn't a long flight. They probably save the bigger planes for the longer flights," Ruby reassured her. She honestly didn't care what the plane looked like by this point. She just wanted to hurry up and board.

Maude looked at the plane and then back over to Ruby. She wasn't completely convinced that this thing would actually make it all the way to Italy. But she'd come too far in this adventure to stay in Istanbul. They boarded the plane and settled in for the flight that would have them in Rome, Italy in three short hours. Maude closed her eyes and vowed to not open them until the plane landed in Italy.

❧Chapter Fifteen❧

Maude clutched the armrest for the twentieth time. It didn't matter that this flight was shorter. She was fully convinced that they had more than doubled the distance with all the bouncing up and down. She looked over at Ruby who was gripping her armrest just as tightly. Beside Ruby, Opal was happily singing while she looked out of the window. Opal seemed to think that the scarier the ride the more exciting the adventure.

"What was that?" Ruby yelped. There was a sudden loud noise followed by smaller, more troubling sounds.

"We probably hit a bird," Opal shrugged. She went back to singing and ignored Maude and Ruby's alarmed looks.

"What?" Ruby squealed.

"Happens all the time," Opal replied like a professional traveler.

Maude ignored them both and continued to think about the sandy beaches and beautiful men that awaited her. Maude's thoughts were interrupted by an announcement from the pilot. He was speaking the same language that she'd heard in the airport. Turkish certainly was a difficult language to understand. It wasn't until he began speaking heavily accented English that Maude became worried.

"Eh, ladies and gentlemens, we are having some troubles with our engines and we will be making an emergency landing in Tirana in Albania in a few minutes. We land very quickly so please put on your seatbelts. Thank you," the pilot said.

"Huh?" Ruby asked. "Opal! What do you see out there?"

"Land, ho, matey!" Opal cheered.

"What?" Ruby yelled. She leaned over Opal to see out the window. "All I see is clouds!" She slapped Opal on the shoulder. Opal doubled over laughing at her joke.

"What did he just say?" Maude asked. She had missed the captain's announcement thanks to Ruby and Opal.

The woman next to Maude patted her on the arm and motioned for her to buckle her seat belt.

"We're in Italy already?" Maude asked.

"No, no," the woman smiled. "Albania."

"We're in Albania?" Maude asked her.

"Yes, yes. We land," the lady nodded kindly, although she didn't seem too confident.

"We're landing? In Albania?" Maude asked.

"Yes, yes," the lady told her. "Bad engine."

Maude glared over at Ruby and Opal. "We're landing in Albania?"

Opal broke out into an impromptu rendition of Come Fly With Me.

"What?" Ruby yelled. "Why?"

"I don't know! Probably because I'm being punished for something I did in a past life!" Maude reeled. "We might as well just jump out of the window and hope we die before we hit the ground."

"Darn, I forgot to pack my parachute!" Opal sighed.

"Shut up you ol' coot!" Maude shouted at her.

"I ain't old!" Opal shot back.

"Why are we landing in Albania?" Ruby asked again.

"Probably because there's smoke coming out of the engine," Opal said.

"There's what?" Maude screeched.

"We're going to die," Ruby said, fanning herself.

"Hush up, Ruby," Maude didn't trust herself to be polite when her life was flashing before her eyes. This was it. This was the moment she was going to die. All before she had ever set foot in Italy.

"This should be fun!" Opal cheered. She made sure her seatbelt was buckled and put both of her arms in the air like she was on a ride at the fair.

"Opal! Put your hands down and hold on!" Ruby scolded her.

They felt like they were afloat on the ocean. The plane rocked from side to side, one wing falling as the other one rose up in the air. Then, out of nowhere, the back of the plane seemed to slide forward before the rocking of the wings began again.

"Ruby, think about it. Is holding on really going to make a difference here?" Opal asked. She laughed and winked at an ashen faced Ruby. Ruby turned to Maude and gulped.

The plane took a sudden turn and Ruby and Maude held onto the armrests for dear life. Maude closed her eyes and vowed not to open them until she saw Saint Peter himself on the other side.

If she survived this, Maude was never, ever flying again. She didn't know what was rocking up and down more: her stomach or the plane. She felt it lurch once more. Ruby was praying loudly and clutching her chest as if she was trying to keep her heart from jumping out of her ribcage. Opal, on the other hand, had no understanding of life or death.

The plane dropped suddenly. "Oh dear God!" Maude panicked. The woman beside her grabbed her hand and they embraced. Maude, who was not a hugger, didn't care that she'd never met this lady before. Maybe a hug would help break the impending crash.

Opal seemed to be the only passenger on the plane that thought they were having a joyride. Most were praying or braced for impact. No one was braced harder than Maude and no one was praying louder than Ruby.

One last yaw and the left wing dipped again. Maude felt the front of the plane rise up. The wings leveled out and then they seemed to be bouncing on a solid surface. Maude fell forward as the brakes began to slow the aircraft.

"You can open your eyes now," Opal said.

Maude timidly opened one eye and looked around. She was not in heaven, nor was she still in the air. She opened her other eye and saw that Opal had appeared right in front of her. She was inches from her nose.

"Geez, Opal! Get out of my face!" Maude gasped.

"Just making sure you're still alive," Opal smiled.

"Oh God! I'm in hell, aren't I?" Maude moaned.

"Nope! Wrong again!" Opal grinned. "We're in the great country of Albania!"

"Where's Albania?" Ruby asked.

"Right here," Opal said. She pointed outside the window and looked at Ruby like she was an idiot. "I literally just told you we were here."

"I may kill her if you don't," Ruby snarled to Maude.

Maude took a deep breath and counted to ten.

"Earth to Maude! Earth to Ruby! Come on!" Opal huffed. She was already on her feet with her arms full of shopping bags. She had her shawl she had bought in Nepal wrapped around her head. "Let's get off."

"Wh-what?" Ruby stammered.

"Let's get off," Opal drawled slowly. "As in off the plane."

Maude looked around at all of the other passengers who were gathering up their belongings. They had made it safely to the ground after all.

"Y'all, come on!" Opal snapped. She was tired of waiting for them to shake themselves out of whatever funk they were in. If they didn't get a move on, they were going to be the last souls on the plane. She handed Ruby her pillow and bags and stepped over her to get to Maude.

"Here, take this. And this. Oh, and this, too. Let's get a move on," Opal directed.

Maude and Ruby stood up and obeyed orders. They followed Opal off the airplane and through the doors to the airport. Maude sank down in the nearest chair and let the pillow and bags fall to the floor.

"I almost died!" she mumbled.

"Well, technically, we didn't almost die," Opal reasoned. "It's not the first time a plane has had to emergency land."

Maude ignored her and shook her head. "I'm never flying again," she promised aloud.

"Well, Maude, we still aren't exactly in Italy, so we're going to have to," Ruby acknowledged.

"I am never flying again!" Maude rounded on Ruby. "I mean it. No more planes for me!"

"We'll see," Opal said.

"We'll see nothing!" Maude muttered. She took the bags and lumbered off.

"She forgot we have to fly home after Italy," Opal smirked.

Ruby shook her head and whispered, "I don't think now is a good time to mention that little tidbit of information." She was watching Maude pace off in the distance.

"Well, how about the tidbit that we still aren't in Italy? What are we supposed to do about that?" Opal asked.

Ruby hadn't thought of that. How exactly were they going to get to Italy now? Ruby didn't think they'd be able to convince Maude to get back on a plane so quickly after this experience.

"There's always a train," Opal suggested.

"I don't think I can handle another train ride," Ruby replied.

Ruby and Opal made their way toward the ticket counter. They left Maude ranting in the little circular path she'd created. Apparently the other passengers thought she was crazy because they all gave her a wide berth.

"I always knew she'd reach her snapping point," Opal sighed. "Oh, how quickly the mighty fall. Sad really."

Ruby ignored Opal and explained the situation as best she could to the young woman behind the counter. Her name tag read Ajola. There was no train that traveled from Tirana to Naples, or Rome for that matter. But there was a ferry that left from Durres, Albania that went to Bari, Italy. They should be able to find transportation to Naples once they arrived in Bari.

"There! Problem solved. Even ol' sour britches over there can't complain about a ferry boat," Opal said.

"Ummm, where exactly is this town where we catch the ferry? This Durrin place?" Ruby asked politely.

"Durres," Ajola corrected her. "It's a town about forty kilometers away. From there you catch the ferry in the morning and cross the strait."

"Ahh, the Strait of Otranto," Opal nodded.

Ajola nodded and smiled. Ruby looked at Opal with wide eyes. How did she know that? It might be the only way. At least they'd be in Italy.

"Is there a bus or anything going to that city?" Ruby asked hopefully.

"Not at this time of night," Ajola answered. "No buses till the morning."

Ruby looked around the airport. Everything was closed. There wasn't even a gift shop open for her to buy a souvenir. She and Opal walked over to the baggage claim area where Maude was still pacing. She explained the situation to a somewhat calmer Maude. Maude mumbled something about probably drowning, but otherwise she was in favor of waiting until morning to catch a bus to meet the ferry. They grabbed their suitcases from the claim area before they settled on a row of benches and tried to get comfortable.

Ruby was thinking about what her parents would say when they heard all about this adventure when the girl from the counter tapped her on the shoulder. The girl, Ajola, was standing beside a much older man.

"Excuse me, but my grandfather say he go to Durres for deliveries. He takes you in his truck, po?" Ajola asked.

"Your grandfather can give us a ride?" Ruby clarified.

"Po. Um, yes," she replied.

The old man nodded. All he kept saying was "po, po."

"Yes, yes. That would be great!" Ruby jumped up and smiled at the girl.

"Pack it up, Maude! We're going on a drive!" Opal cheered. She wondered why the man mentioned the police, but she knew better than to ask. Hopefully they'd be able to keep the police out of this matter.

Maude was already gathering the bags. "Lead the way," she told Ruby.

They followed Ajola and her grandfather out of the airport through one of the service doors. They soon learned that this leg of their journey would be on the back of a produce delivery truck. Maude was mumbling something under her breath as she lifted the bags up to Opal who was the first to jump on board.

"This is going to be great!" Opal yelled. "It's like our own personal hayride!"

When Ruby and Maude had climbed up and joined Opal, the old man shut the back gate of the truck.

"Po, po," he said again as he nodded to each of the ladies.

The canvas cover did little to keep the chill out, but at least they were getting that much closer to

Italy. If they could just get on the ferry in the morning, then they might actually make it there.

Opal bit into a stray tomato. "Wow, this is delicious!"

"Let me guess," Maude said. "Tastes like chicken." She rolled her eyes and mumbled something about life not being fair.

"No, Maude, it tastes like a tomato," Opal replied. She could not believe how naive Maude was.

Maude picked up a rotten tomato that had rolled beside her foot and threw it at Opal.

"Hey! What was that for?" Opal yelled.

"For being a nimwit!" Maude retorted.

"Y'all hush!" Ruby scolded. "You're embarrassing me!"

Except for a loud burp out of Opal, the rest of the ride was smooth and silent. Ruby thanked Ajole's grandfather, Agron, profusely when they arrived at the dock.

"Thank you, thank you, thank you!" Ruby exclaimed as Opal tossed their belongings down to Maude.

"Po!" Agron said. "Lamtumirë!" He smiled and hopped back into his truck. The girls waved to him as he rounded the corner.

"Now what?" Maude asked. It was pitch black outside, except for a few streetlamps by the dock.

"I reckon we sit a spell and wait for the ferry," Opal smiled. It was hard to see in the dim lighting, but the bench by the dock looked sturdy enough for them to sit. "Ahh, and now we wait."

"Wait for what exactly?" Maude asked.

"Fate," Opal replied.

Maude nor Ruby liked the sound of that.

∽Chapter Sixteen∾

Maude awoke to a strange man tapping her on her shoulder. She looked around to see her two best friends huddled together on the bench.

"Can I help you?" she mumbled.

The man pointed to the small ferry behind her. With an overly animated smile, he motioned for her to get up and move to the ferry.

"Give me a minute," she yawned. She stretched her arms high over her head and wished she had saved another rotten tomato to throw at Opal to wake her up.

"Rise and shine," she yelled.

Ruby roused immediately and adjusted her eyes to the soft light peeking in from the rising sun. "Is it time to board?" she asked sleepily.

"Apparently," Maude replied. The man was still pointing at Maude and back again to the ferry. "Wake up Opal and let's go before this guy has a fit."

Ruby gently poked Opal who shrugged her off. She then began poking her harder until finally Opal opened her eyes and looked around. She jumped to her feet and said, "let's go!"

"I don't know how she does that," Ruby whispered to Maude. "Freaks me out every time."

Ruby and Maude grabbed their things and followed behind Opal and the man to the ferry.

"You remember that ol' ferry boat they used to have to cross the Moccasin River?" Maude asked Ruby.

"Sure wasn't anything like this, was it?" Ruby replied.

Ruby wasn't exactly sure what she had expected when they told her about the ferry, but she certainly wasn't expecting a fancy ship like this. There was a line of cars driving on the boat to board. Passengers, such as herself, were lined up around the building. She honestly didn't know how any boat, even one as big as the one she was looking at, would hold that many people. But hold them it did. As a matter of fact, it held many, many more. They bought their tickets and joined the long line.

Once they boarded the ferry, they found a table in the cafe on the upper deck.

"This is really nice," Maude looked around approvingly.

Ruby agreed. She had never been on a boat like this before. She overheard the woman next to her say that it would take almost eleven hours to get to Bari. She thought it best to keep that information to herself and not share it with Maude or Opal.

"Hey, earth to Ruby!" Opal said, bringing Ruby out of her daydream. "What do you want to eat?"

They each ordered a croissant with jam. Ruby and Maude ordered coffee. Opal, being the only one who didn't regularly drink coffee, ordered a hot tea of some kind.

"This water sure is beautiful. Not exactly good for surfing, but fine nonetheless," Opal said.

"What do you know about surfing? You ain't never been surfing a day in your life!" Maude retorted.

"I'm just saying!" Opal replied. "And I wasn't aware you know everything about me."

"You have to admit that Opal is always full of surprises," Ruby nudged Maude. Even Maude had to laugh at that.

They finished breakfast and relaxed for a few minutes while they sipped on their drinks. The dining area was filling up rapidly, so they decided to find seats elsewhere on the boat.

"What's wrong Ruby? Feeling a little seasick?" Opal asked.

"No, I'm ok. I'm just a little bummed that the gift shops were closed in the airport. I really wanted a souvenir to remember our time in Albania," she replied.

"A crick in your neck from napping on that bench isn't enough? What about the stains in your pants from the near death experience of that flight?" Maude laughed.

Ruby laughed, but she still wanted a set of shirts to commemorate this leg of their adventure. After exploring for a few minutes, Ruby's eyes lit up. There in the corner was a dingy, out of the way gift shop. It wasn't exactly a shop per se. It was more like a counter with a few shirts and trinkets, but Ruby was overjoyed and practically bounced over to see what they had in stock.

"I've never seen someone so happy to buy a cheap shirt," Maude said, shaking her head.

"Maybe she should have packed more like I did," Opal replied.

Maude looked at her. For a moment she thought about reminding Opal that she and Ruby had packed for her, but then she remembered the crash landing and praying to God for intervention. She'd made a brief promise to God about controlling her temper. She figured she should at least try to hold up her end of the bargain since she had survived and all.

"Mine eyes have seen the glory!" Ruby exclaimed. She unloaded her shopping bags into the Maude's lap. "I found us matching shirts!"

"Shocker," Maude said under her breath.

"Is that the Albanian flag?" Opal asked.

"I think so!" Ruby squealed with delight.

"You don't know?" Maude asked in a shocked tone.

"Well, there's a language barrier, Maude!" Ruby replied haughtily. "Here. Take this shirt and put it on over the one you're wearing. We can all match once we get to Italy!"

"Okay," Maude relented. She pulled the shirt on and held up her arms for Ruby's inspection. "Can we go find us a place to sit down now?"

Many of the seats were already filled, but they managed to find two benches facing each other in one of the corners of the passenger cabin.

"This looks perfect," Ruby said, dropping her bag in the seat.

Maude unloaded the bags against the wall and sat down on the edge of the bench. Ruby and Opal faced opposite her.

"How long does it take to get to Body?" Maude asked.

"Body? Whose body are we going to?" Ruby asked.

"No, Body in Italy. Or wherever this boat is taking us," Maude replied.

"Not Body, you uncultured moose. Bari, like sorry. Like you're sorry for being an old goat," Opal explained.

"Yes, Bari," Ruby explained. "At least that's how Ajola pronounced it."

"That's what I said. How long does it take to get to Bari?" Maude asked again.

Ruby looked over at Opal and shook her head ever so slightly.

"What am I missing?" Maude asked.

"Um, it's a little over ten hours on the ferry. So we've got about eight hours left to go," Ruby winced.

"WHAT?" Maude yelled.

That was exactly what Ruby was afraid of. "Maude, calm down," Ruby tried to diffuse the situation, but she knew it was no use.

"Calm down? Calm down! How can I calm down? I don't even know how many airplanes I've been on, how many different countries I've been in, how many steps I've taken since we left Rhinestone. I honestly couldn't even tell you where we are on a map right now. Shut up Opal, I don't need your help!" Maude yelled.

Opal zipped her lips and melted into her seat.

Maude was just getting started. "You see, I can't calm down Ruby. I am exhausted and hungry and exhausted," she paused for a breath.

"You said exhausted twice," Opal pointed out.

Maude silenced her with a glare. "My point is that I am beyond exasperated with all of this and all of you," Maude said through gritted teeth. She was pacing in front of them.

"Are you finished?" Ruby asked her.

"As a matter of fact, no. When has it ever been a good idea for anyone to tell a woman to calm down?" Maude asked. "After everything we've been through on this trip, you expect me to be happy about an all day ferry ride?"

Maude crossed her arms over her chest. The other two watched her for a minute.

"Ok. Now I'm finished," Maude huffed.

Ruby waited for her to sit down before she began. "For your information, Maude, you haven't exactly been a peach either. Opal and I are both exhausted and worn out. We have both walked the same amount of steps that you have, flown the same amount of miles that you have, and traversed all the countries that you have. We're somewhere in the middle of some sea between Albania and Italy. Do you think this is how I thought I would spend my summer? Absolutely not! Do you think this is even remotely fun for me out here in some godforsaken sea and some boat that could capsize at any minute? Do you think I wanna drown in the middle of some body of water I don't even know the name of? I didn't ask for any of this, neither did Opal. But at least we aren't groaning and complaining every five seconds like you are. None of us can help what's been done so far, but you can help your attitude."

"Damn Ruby," Opal said. She didn't finish that thought because Ruby cut her eyes at her next.

A few minutes of silence passed when Maude spoke up. "I'm sorry Ruby. And I'm sorry Opal. I know y'all are tired and worn out, too. I'm just ready to get the best summer of our lives started," she said.

Ruby nodded and patted Maude's knee. "I forgive you," she smiled.

"Hey, I was thinking earlier about something and I don't want y'all getting all huffy again, but what if it still is the best summer of our lives?" Opal said.

"What do you mean?" Ruby asked.

"I mean, what if all of this craziness is all part of it! Just look at all the places we've been and all the things we've seen. No one in Rhinestone will ever believe the adventures we've been on! All the new food and people and adventures! It's all part of it!" Opal said.

Maude nodded and Ruby's jaw dropped. They were amazed at what Opal was saying. Opal was right. It really was all part of their adventurous summer. No one in Rhinestone had ever experienced the things that they already had.

"And the adventures aren't over," Opal continued. "We aren't even in Italy yet! We haven't experienced Italy and all that it has to offer."

"You're right," Maude said. She was suddenly feeling much better. "Let's make the best of this!" She high-fived Opal and went to high-five Ruby, but quickly pulled her hand back when she saw Ruby's face. "You ok, Ruby?"

Ruby shook her head and put her hand to her mouth. She barely made it to the rail before she got sick.

"Well, can't exactly make the best of that, can ya?" Opal said.

Maude had to agree with her on that one. "Let's give her some breathing room. The rocking of these waves must be getting to her," Maude said.

She and Opal scooped up the bags and deposited them into a set of chairs further down the stretch. They could still keep an eye on Ruby without having to hear her vomit over the rails.

As the day stretched on, Ruby started to feel better. She rinsed out her mouth with some water and changed into her new shirt. "Ok, I'm good now," she said.

"There it is!" cried Opal suddenly. She leaned over the railing and pointed off into the distance. "I see Italy!"

Maude squinted her eyes and could just make out the edge of something far off in the distance. Ruby began to jump up and down. "I see it, too!" she exclaimed.

They stayed at the railing and watched as Italy came into view right before their eyes. It was a magnificent sight to behold. Gigantic limestone buildings jutted directly out of the massive boulders along the sea. From a distance, it was impossible to tell where the man made structures began and where God's creation ended. Ruby was in awe of the sight. For once Opal was completely speechless. Even Maude couldn't fully take in the beauty they were seeing. Eventually, she was able to utter, "wow," to which the others only nodded in agreement.

When the ferry finally made it to the dock, they couldn't wait to step out onto Italian soil.

"We made it!" Maude cheered. "Finally!"

Opal began to dance a little jig and for the first time on the entire expedition, Maude joined in.

"Benvenuto a Italia!" a rosy faced man said as they disembarked from the boat. "Benvenuti a Bari, casa di San Nicola!"

"San Nicola?" Maude asked him.

"Saint Nicholas!" he said with a thick Italian accent.

"Saint Nicholas? The Saint Nicholas?" Opal asked. She pushed Maude out of the way to reach the man. "The jolliest saint there ever was?"

The man laughed heartily and nodded, "Si, si. San Nicola, si!"

"What is she going on about?" Ruby asked Maude.

Opal quickly turned around and rushed over to Maude and Ruby. "It's Santa Claus! The real Santa Claus!" she shrieked. "Oh my goodness. I'm going to meet the real Santa Claus! Oh my goodness. How's my hair?"

"How's your hair?" Maude asked. "It looks as good as it's gonna get." Maude turned to Ruby and explained, "That man told her that Bari was the home of Saint Nicholas and this little elf is losing her mind," Maude explained.

Ruby laughed and congratulated Opal. "I know you've waited your whole life for this moment," she smiled.

"Oh my goodness. Oh gosh," Opal stammered. "Santa Claus. The REAL Santa Claus. And I didn't even bring my Christmas list!"

Opal walked with a new bounce in her step through the streets of Bari. She practically danced up the charming streets, commenting every now and again about the old buildings that lined them.

"She's going to hyperventilate," Ruby told Maude.

"Probably," Maude nodded. "I've never seen her this excited about anything."

"San Nicola," Ruby said. "I like the way it rolls off the tongue."

"San Nicola? Laggiù," a man said after overhearing the Americans. He pointed down the street and Opal took off at a brisk pace.

"Opal! Where are you going?" Maude yelled after her.

Ruby shrugged her shoulders and the two of them hurried after Opal carrying all of the suitcases and bags. It did not take them long to find her. Opal was standing in front of a large sign that was printed in Italian and English stating that the remains of San Nicola, Saint Nicolas, were just through the doors.

"Are we going inside?" Maude asked Opal.

"It's a fake!" Opal said. She shook her head and grimaced. "He said it was Santa Claus, but Santa ain't dead. They didn't even get his beard right in the pictures!"

"But," Maude began.

Maude looked at Ruby who shook her head. "Let it be," she whispered.

"Um, right. Ok. Let's head to the train station and get out of this, um, fake Santa city," Maude said. Ruby nodded her head and encouraged Maude to continue. "What do you say, Opal? Maude asked.

Opal shrugged her shoulders and agreed to follow them back through the maze like roads to the train station. A good bit of the spring in her step was gone. She couldn't believe it. These people were passing this off as the home of Santa Claus and they didn't even know what he looked like.

~Chapter Seventeen~

Ruby was the first to realize that they were lost wandering the streets of Bari. They walked along the maze like streets until Ruby decided it might be best to ask for directions.

"I'm hungry. Ask for some directions to some good eats," Maude said.

"I could eat, too," Opal admitted. She was feeling extremely let down still by the pseudo Santa.

"Let's find somewhere quick then," Ruby said. She was ready to get on the train to Rome and then figure out how they would get to Naples. Naples is where she could immerse herself in the true Italian culture.

Ruby dug through her bag and pulled out the little English-Italian dictionary that she had picked up at the gift shop in New York. She had anticipated using it much sooner, but at least she was finally getting the chance to use it now.

"Scusi," she said to the two old men who were sitting on a bench playing chess. "Do-vee ristorante?"

"Ristorante?" the balding gentleman asked.

"Si, si," Ruby nodded vigorously.

"Vieni con me. Conosco un posto magnifico," he stood up and began to walk down the street.

"Oh, are we supposed to follow him?" Ruby asked.

Opal was already trotting along beside the man, chatting away.

"Looks like it. Let's go," Maude told Ruby.

"Magnifico, magnifico," he turned and told Ruby again.

"He said it's magnificent," Opal turned back to them and translated.

"Yeah, I figured that much out on my own," Maude muttered.

They turned a few more times before he stopped outside a small building with vines crawling upward across a large window.

"Mio cognato possiede questo ristorante. Trattoria," he told Opal.

"Si! Trattoria," Opal repeated to Maude and Ruby.

"What in the world is that?" Maude asked Ruby who was frantically looking through her dictionary.

"It means we'll love it," Opal replied.

"Is that what it means?" Maude whispered to Ruby.

Ruby shrugged. Her travel dictionary wasn't prepared for someone who spoke so quickly.

"Of course it does," Opal said. She rolled her eyes at her friends.

"When'd you learn to speak Italian?" Maude asked her.

"It's one of my many hidden talents," Opal smirked.

Ruby gave up looking for it. "Grazie," she said as she nodded to the old man.

"Prego," he replied. He waved at someone through the window and moments later, a handsome man rushed out and kissed him on both cheeks. They broke into an animated discussion before the stranger turned to them and motioned them inside.

"I'm glad he didn't decide to kiss us," Ruby said.

"I don't know. He's kinda cute," Opal replied.

"He's old enough to be your grandfather!" Maude stared at her.

"Yeah, he probably is too old then," Opal agreed.

"What kind of food does this place have?" Maude asked.

"Italian," Opal said seriously.

"You don't say," she replied sarcastically. "I meant like do they have chicken, beef, pizza?"

"Pizza?" Opal gasped. "Pizza? Maude! You embarrass me with your lack of culinary knowledge. You can't order pizza in a nice ristorante like this."

Ruby looked back at the two of them squabbling like children. "Are y'all coming?"

"Ruby! Maude says she's going to order pizza!" Opal exclaimed.

"Did not! I asked if they had it, is all," Maude retorted.

"What's the big deal?" Ruby asked Opal.

"I'm surrounded by cultural bozos," Opal lamented. She looked at Maude and Ruby and shook her head. "You can't order pizza in Italy. They see that as such a tacky touristy thing. It's offensive!"

"Oh no, Maude! You can't have pizza then," Ruby said. She immediately sided with Opal on this argument.

"I never said, oh, never mind," Maude huffed.

"Don't worry, I'll order for us. I've got this," Opal assured them.

"Oh God," Maude whispered to Ruby. They followed their new friend inside the charming trattoria and sat down at a table underneath a high window.

"Bene?" the man asked.

"Molto bene, Antonio!" Opal said with a smile. Antonio kissed Opal on her cheek and turned to do the same to Maude who instantly put her hand up to stop him.

"Thanks, but um," Maude started to say.

"Maude!" Ruby hissed. She had turned a deep shade of crimson after Antonio bestowed kisses on her cheeks and walked back outside.

"I love Italy!" Opal declared.

"Me, too!" Ruby agreed. "Speaking of that, we need to find some t-shirts that say that. Gotta keep up tradition!"

"Ciao! My name is Francesco," a voice above them said. It was the handsome man who greeted Antonio earlier.

"H-hi," Maude stuttered. She certainly wouldn't mind a good old fashioned greeting from this man.

Francesco smiled warmly at her before smiling at Ruby and Opal.

"My grandfather says you are ready to dine with us here today. He was quite charmed by you, signora," he said to Opal. Opal smiled and winked at Maude and Ruby. "I was told to bring by a bottle of our best vino to begin with our antipasti. Do you know by chance what you would like to order next?"

Maude and Ruby both looked at Opal with baited breath.

"Risotto e gnocchi, grazie. E poi pollo, pesce, e manzo. Insalatas e gorgonzola," Opal smiled.

"Molto bene, Opal!" Francesco cheered. "Not bad. I will bring the vino and get those to the cucina." Francesco turned on his heels and hurried off to the kitchen.

"You can stop staring now," Opal laughed. Maude's eyes had not left the handsome waiter's behind.

"Huh?" Maude said. She had missed Opal's entire order because she could not stop staring at how good looking this man was.

"He is cute," Ruby giggled. "Golly, look at this view!"

For the first time, the three women looked out the window at the crowds passing by.

"It's so cute here. Can you believe it! We are in Italy!" Ruby said.

Francesco brought out wine glasses and a bottle of wine that was a deep red color. He poured the wine and Maude took a large gulp.

"No, no, you must pace yourself," Francesco stopped her. "Softly, gently," he smiled.

"Maude gulped again and dribbled wine down the front of her shirt, Her eyes had still not left Francesco's.

"Maude! You're embarrassing me!" Ruby whispered.

Francesco handed Maude another cloth napkin and walked back towards the kitchen. Maude sipped the wine and closed her eyes. "This is divine," she said.

Ruby and Opal couldn't help but smirk at Maude's crush. They passed the time oohing and ahhing at the villagers who passed in and out of the beautiful trattoria. They devoured the appetizers of fruit and bruschetta. They were already feeling quite full when Francesco and a young woman brought out their trays of food. Ruby's eyes widened at the mounds of food.

"Ok, we have chicken, fish, and beef. Ruby?" Opal asked.

"I think I'll stick with the chicken," she replied.

"You're sure it's beef?" Maude whispered.

Opal silenced her with one look. She handed Maude the platter of beef and took the plate of fish for herself. It all smelled heavenly.

It did not take long for them to fill up on the courses of a true Italian feast. They couldn't eat another bite. This had by far been the best meal of their trip. Francesco kept the vino coming long after they had pushed their plates away.

Suddenly, Francesco appeared before them with three custard dishes.

"For my new American friends," he gushed.

"What's this?" Ruby asked. Maybe she had room for just one more bite.

"Zabaglione," Francesco said smiling. "Our special family recipe. Delizioso!"

Opal wasted no time. She took the biscotti and began dipping it into the custard. "Mmmm," she purred. "Maude, you've gotta try this!"

Maude, who was naturally more cautious than Opal, looked the dish over for a minute before following Opal's lead. Ruby was too busy eating her dessert to worry about the other two.

"This is amazing! What's in it?" Ruby asked.

Francesco smiled coyly. "Special family recipe. Mama never tells anyone," he grinned. He turned towards Ruby and leaned in closer to her and whispered, "But, it's the amaretto that gives it the special flavor." Ruby blushed a deep shade of red and Francesco grinned. Maude crossed her arms and frowned. Francesco left them to their dessert and walked back to the kitchen.

"I love Italy!" Opal said. She'd devoured the biscotti. She looked over at Maude who was now raising the custard dish to her lips to drink the rest of her dessert.

"Don't you dare!" Ruby scolded her.

"What?" Maude asked innocently.

"You have no couth," Opal told her.

"Shh! Both of y'all stop. Opal, you're one to talk!" Ruby whispered.

"I'm just as couth as you are. Maybe even couther!" Opal countered.

"Couther ain't a word," Maude told her.

"Maybe it is and maybe it isn't!" Opal said defiantly.

"This was amazing. I hate to leave," Ruby said.

"I know. Me too. But I guess we need to get to the train station so we can get to Rome," Maude told her.

"Roma! Is molto bello," Francesco said. He had reappeared behind them suddenly.

"Molto bello?" Ruby asked.

"Very beautiful. Like you," he said.

Maybe it was the vino or the richness of the dessert, but Ruby suddenly felt flush. "Thank you," she mumbled.

Maude looked put out as she pushed her chair noisily under the table. She followed Opal outside and looked around. "Now what?" she asked.

"Ruby's paying the check and getting directions to the train station," Opal replied. "Maybe she's getting his address, too, because that man is built like a marble statue. Lord almighty, he is handsome!"

"Of course she is," Maude grumbled.

"Relax, Maude. We're in Italy! There's gorgeous people all around us. Let Ruby have this one. It's good to keep her mind off Jameson," Opal reminded her.

Opal was right. This was a good thing. "Ok, you're right. But I call the next gorgeous man," Maude smiled.

Ruby emerged from the restaurant a few minutes later with red cheeks and a smile that lit up her entire face. "Ok, we're close to the station. Just a few blocks up this way."

"Smile compliments of your new friend?" Opal asked slyly.

"Oh hush," Ruby smiled brighter. "He's a real gentleman. He's very kind and said if we ever make it back here to Bari, to look him up."

"I bet he'd like that," Opal whispered and nudged Ruby's arm.

"He also said that his uncle owns a hostel in Rome. Francesco is going to call him and make sure we have a place to stay once we get to Rome." Ruby smiled.

"Oh, he's introducing you to his family. That's a big step," Opal said knowingly.

Ruby rolled her eyes and directed them in the direction of the station.

When they arrived at the train station, Ruby bought the tickets and they waited for an hour for the next train to Rome. Opal made friends with fellow travelers and Maude dozed off, still full from the delicious feast that was catching up to her.

When the train arrived at the station, they immediately saw how different it was from the train they rode in India. This train was sleek and looked brand new. There were no sleeping cars available on this train as the entire trip would only take four hours. They settled into a crowded car and found an empty row of seats by the window.

The rocking of the train against the track coupled with the nice meal and a few too many glasses of vino had the three young women asleep before they could see the rain clouds form in the distant sky.

All too soon, Maude felt a tap on her shoulder. She looked up to see the porter smiling down at her.

"Siamo a Roma," he said.

"Huh?" Maude asked.

"Roma," he said again, but louder this time. He pointed out the window. "Roma."

Maude woke Opal and Ruby. "Hey you two, wake up. We're here."

She grabbed the bags and the three of them made their way down to the platform.

"So, how do we get to this hostel that your new boyfriend booked for us?" Maude asked.

Ruby wasn't sure how to answer. She had been a little too smitten with her temporary suitor to get all of the details. Now she was kicking herself for not asking him.

"Maybe we can ask the guy with the sign over there," Opal laughed.

They all turned to see a young man holding a sign that read, "Rube, Opall, e Mode."

"Geez, are all the people beautiful here?" Maude asked with her mouth slightly open.

"Oh my," Ruby stammered. "That's his uncle?"

"He's mine!" Opal said.

"He looks younger than Francesco! Can't be his uncle, but I'll ask," Maude said. She shoved her way through the crowd to get closer to him. No doubt about it, they all loved Italy!

"Ciao!" Maude waved to the young man. She smiled and nearly melted when he laughed.

"You have a, something right there," he replied and pointed to her teeth.

Maude turned red faced and turned her back to him. "Is there something in my teeth?" she demanded to know. Opal nodded and whispered, "I thought you were saving it for later." Opal shrugged and pushed her out of the way.

"Ciao, amico!" Opal smiled. "Francesco zio?"

"No, no. Cugino. Ahh, Rube?" he asked.

Ruby smiled and waved at him. "I'm Ruby," she replied.

"Ah, Rube!" he smiled. He descended on her with the traditional cheek kisses and turned to Opal. "Opal e Mode?"

"Opal!" she sang.

He kissed her and turned to Maude. "Mode?"

"Maude," she replied quietly. She was careful not to expose her teeth too much.

"Perfetto! I'm Niccolo, Francesco's cugino. My papa, Tomasso, sent me here for you," he explained.

"Great! Let's go!" Opal said. She linked arms with Niccolo and left Maude and Ruby to follow with the bags.

⌒Chapter Eighteen⌒

Tommaso and his wife Gabriella owned a beautiful hostel in the middle of the city. Ruby, Maude, and Opal fell asleep instantly after following Niccolo through the winding streets of Rome. They were so exhausted and well fed that they were asleep the moment their heads hit the pillows.

Opal was the first to wake up the next morning. She tried to stay quiet and let Maude and Ruby sleep, but she was too excited.

"Rise and shine!" she called out. Ruby opened her eyes slowly and yawned deeply. Maude merely turned over with a grunt.

Opal jumped on top of Maude's bunk and started patting her exposed shoulder. "Rise and shine, Mode!" she giggled.

"Get off me," Maude snapped.

"Only if you hurry up and get dressed. We've got things to do, my friend!" Opal sang cheerfully. She was already dressed. "Here, I'll find you some clothes."

Maude grunted again and rolled over to face Opal who was already digging through Maude's suitcase. "Here, put on these pants and this shirt. It's decent enough," Opal said. She threw the outfit at Maude. "You need help, Ruby?"

"I think I can manage," Ruby laughed. She stood up and stretched before grabbing her own suitcase. She found a light blue shirt near the top and pulled it on over her unbrushed hair. "Probably should have tried this on before I bought it. It's a little tight, but that's ok. I need to brush my teeth and attempt to look more like a human before we go out."

Opal nodded and sat on the bottom bunk. She had been ready for half an hour already and was getting impatient. "Maude, come on," she whined. "We can sleep when we're dead!"

"Alright, ugh," moaned Maude. "You're always so pushy."

Opal smiled and tapped her foot on the floor. She had the entire day planned for them. She just knew they were going to love her plans. Niccolo had given her a list of places to visit. She was headed to the Trevi Fountain first. Niccolo told her that the fountain was lucky and she wanted to make sure they started the day with as much good luck as possible.

"Ok, I'm ready," Ruby said. She had slept well, but she was still feeling really tired. "I'd like to stop by some shops and maybe a few museums today."

"Sure, sure," Opal muttered. "Where's Mode, I mean Maude?"

"She was still in the bathroom when I left. I think she's trying to catch a glimpse of Niccolo," Ruby laughed.

"He's already at work," Opal said matter of factly. "He stopped by earlier while y'all were sawing logs and said goodbye."

"Oh great!" Ruby huffed.

Maude came back in looking much more refreshed than she had in the past few days. "Alright, where to?" she smiled.

"We're doing all the things!" Opal exclaimed. "First, La Fontana di Trevi."

Opal's excitement was contagious. Ruby and Maude were both caught up in it.

"Alright, let's do it!" Maude said.

"How do we get there?" Ruby asked.

"Niccolo said there was a place to rent vespas right outside," Opal explained.

"Perfect!" said Ruby.

A light breeze was blowing through the morning air. It was almost as hot as a July day in Rhinestone, but somehow the heat was more exotic here. This was Italy after all. They were in Rome, exploring the city, and traveling the world. It was exhilarating to simply walk down these streets that had been here for centuries. No one else in Rhinestone could say that they had been to Italy. The most exciting thing anyone from Rhinestone had ever done was travel to Atlanta to visit the Macy's store downtown. Not that Macy's wasn't exciting in its own right, but it certainly wasn't Rome, Italy!

Maude was not certain about the vespa at first, but with a little coaxing from Ruby and a shove from Opal, she was on her way! She didn't want to admit it right away, but she was actually having a good time. She turned her head just in time to see Opal pass by her with her hands in the air. Opal was a daredevil through and through. Maude saw Ruby out of the corner of her eye and urged the vespa to go quicker. There was no way she was going to let Ruby beat her!

They had the best time riding the vespas down the tiny alleyways and through the markets. Maude had to stop on a dime when Opal suddenly came to a halt. Maude swore she heard Ruby curse behind her as she too had to slam on the brakes.

"Opal! What in the sam hill are you doing?" Maude screeched.

"Look!" Opal cried. She pointed to a sign hanging above a rundown looking shop that read "Antiquariato Storico."

"What does that say?" Maude asked.

"Historical antiques!" Opal squealed.

"Ooh, Maude. Let's go in!" Ruby squealed.

"Great. Another gift shop," Maude huffed.

"I bet they have some great deals," Opal said to Ruby.

"Opal, that don't look right," Maude replied. But it was too late. Opal and Ruby had already entered through the shabby looking shop. One of the front windows had a large hole near the top and the glass was shattered in another pane. The glass was too murky and thick to see through completely. The door creaked shut behind her. Maude looked over her shoulder to see if anyone else was around.

"They're going to get themselves killed," Maude said. "Probably already being boiled in a stew by now." She entered through the creaky door and held her breath. The smell of rotten tomatoes and putrid garlic was overpowering. Opal and Ruby were standing at a wooden counter. An old hunchbacked man was behind the counter and gave them a toothless grin.

"Benvenuti amici!" he said.

Maude and Ruby hung back behind Opal who smiled and began to converse in Italian with the old man. "Where did she learn to speak Italian again?" Maude asked Ruby.

Ruby shrugged her shoulders and answered, "She's always full of surprises."

The old man disappeared through a faded curtain behind the counter. "Ooh! This is so exciting! He said he's bringing out a real treasure," Opal said.

"Who?" Maude asked. "The murderer?"

"He's not a murderer! His name is Hector and he's very sweet. He said he's bringing out some china that used to be the Pope's," Opal replied.

"There's no way the Pope is anywhere within a ten mile radius of this place," Maude whispered. "Besides, why do you care what plates the Pope ate on. You ain't even Catholic!"

Opal ignored Maude and leaned over the counter to get a better look at the dusty shelves behind the counter. "Look at this Ruby! The sign says it's an old sword from the Coliseum. And here's a scroll from the time of Christ. We struck the goldmine here!" Opal said.

"Here's an old box of coins! They look a little funny, but what a deal!" Ruby said. Opal and Ruby gushed over the shelves full of random knickknacks that we were clearly fake.

"Bet it was made in China," Maude grumbled.

"Hush up, Maude. He's got some good stuff here," Opal told her.

Maude caught Ruby's attention and gave her a knowing look.

"Here we go!" Opal said excitedly. Hector returned holding a package in his trembling hands.

"Il Papa!" he said happily. He set the package on the counter and slowly unwrapped it.

"Oh, this is a goldmine!" Opal squealed. She handed the plate inside to Ruby who did not share Opal's excitement.

"It's chipped," she said.

"Very good!" Hector clapped. "You want?"

"Um, no thank you," Ruby replied. She handed the plate back to Hector who frowned.

"Why not?" Opal asked. "It's the Pope's favorite plate."

"Opal, the Pope never ate off this piece of crap. It's a fake," Maude said.

"No, no," Hector interjected. "Il Papa."

Maude rolled her eyes and motioned for Opal and Ruby to follow her back outside, but Opal and Ruby stayed put at the counter. "Y'all, come on!"

"Wait, let's see what else he has," Ruby said.

Hector pulled out a box from behind the counter and handed it to Ruby. He smiled broadly.

"What is it?" Ruby asked.

"Dal Vesuvio," Hector explained.

"Vesuvius! He said they're from Vesuvius, Ruby!" Opal clapped.

"Wow! Look Maude!" Ruby said happily. "I've always wanted to see Vesuvius and Pompeii!"

"Si, Pompeii," Hector said.

"Ruby! Opal! That ain't nothing but an old rock from any garden. You can get a basketful out there on the road!" Maude yelled.

Opal smiled at Hector and turned her back to him to face Maude. "Maude, shh. You'll hurt his feelings. He's showing us some real artifacts here," she hissed.

"Ho la croce del Papa," Hector said solemnly.

"No!" Opal cried.

"What'd he say?" Ruby asked.

"He said he has the Pope's cross! Holy cannoli!" Opal said.

Hector pulled a cross necklace from beneath his moth eaten robe and smiled. "Oh my heavens, the Pope's cross," Opal said.

"Where's the Pope?" Maude asked, looking around. "I know he ain't saying he's the Pope."

"Il Papa," Hector said proudly.

"Did he just say he was the Pope?" Ruby asked. She looked at Maude and they both began to howl in laughter. Opal shot them a look and crossed herself. She tried to hide her excitement as she dug through her purse, but Maude snatched it from her before she could find any money.

"Hey!" Opal yelled. "What's the big idea?"

"He's a fraud, Opal. You aren't paying this fool a dime," Maude snapped. She glared at the old man who merely smiled at her.

Maude rolled her eyes again and snatched Opal and Ruby by the arm. "Let's go," she ordered. She ushered Ruby and Opal out of the dingy shop. Thankfully their vespas were still there. Opal looked sullen and refused to look at Maude or Ruby.

"He was a con artist, Opal," Ruby said gently.

"Well, he said he was the Pope," Opal replied.

"Then I'm the Queen of England!" Maude roared. She powered up the vespa and took off. It was time for her to take the lead if they were ever going to cross items off of their lists.

Opal and Ruby followed suit and kept pace behind Maude. They finally made it to the Trevi Fountain where Ruby marveled at the sheer beauty of the statues. People were crowded all around smiling and taking photographs in front of the water. Maude walked around until she found a spot to slip through. It wasn't until she heard a collective gasp followed by laughter that she realized Opal and Ruby were not behind her.

"Oh God," she gasped. Opal had either fallen or jumped into the fountain. She stood up and threw out coins in all directions. Ruby made her way through the crowd to Maude's side and they both tried to flag down Opal.

Opal waded over to them and the crowd parted. "What are you doing?" Maude hissed.

"Niccolo said the fountain was lucky! He said to throw coins in and it would bring me luck," she explained.

Maude and Ruby pulled Opal out of the fountain and Opal shook the water from her hair. "What were you thinking?" Maude demanded again.

"Niccolo said if you throw one coin in the fountain, it means you'll come back to Rome one day. Then he said if you throw two coins you can fall in love and three coins means you'll get married! Or something like that," she shrugged.

"How many did you throw in?" Ruby asked.

"I don't know," Opal said. "A few handfuls just to be on the safe side."

"Probably a good idea, honestly. Oh, Maude, it's fine. Opal has an affinity for water and good luck charms," Ruby said.

"Now that you're done being a mermaid, can we get you dried off and get something to eat?" Maude asked.

"I want to get to at least one museum while we're here. Who knows when we'll ever be back somewhere so pretty," Ruby said.

"Oh, we'll be back!" Opal said. "I threw enough coins in the fountain to make sure of that."

⌐Chapter Nineteen⌐

"I smell food!" Maude whispered.

Opal was finally dry enough to walk without leaving a trail of water behind her. She shook her head like a dog after a bath and squeezed the hem of her dress out on top of Maude's shoes, but the wafting smell of sweet pastries and decadent bread quickly erased Maude's annoyance.

They walked back to their vespas quickly. "Ok, follow me," Ruby said. "The Chapel isn't far."

Ruby was anxious to check items off her bucket list, but Maude had other plans.

"I swear I smell food," Maude said. "I can't possibly go another step without something to eat."

"You always smell food," Opal said. "You got a nose like a bloodhound."

"Hush up," Maude told her.

"Let's get going to the museums or the Sistine. We can always eat later," Ruby said.

"I'm not hungry later. I'm hungry now. And I know I smell some fresh bread and some kind of sugar," Maude said firmly.

"Fine. Let's find Maude's fresh bread," Opal offered.

"Fine," Ruby said grudgingly.

They parked their vespas in front of a large open air marketplace and followed Maude's nose down a small street which opened up into a larger marketplace. Maude quickly made her way to the nearest stall.

"Oh! Look at the rows of fruit and vegetables. They are so cute!" Ruby squealed.

"We did not come all the way to Italy for you to eat fruit, Ruby," Maude sneered. "You can have a pastry or something. Lay off the diet for the next few days."

"I'm not on a diet," Ruby scoffed. "I'm just trying to stay healthy. My stomach has been all over the place lately."

"Exactly. One of these will cure anything you've got," Maude said. She handed Ruby a large flaky pastry with powdered sugar on top.

"No thanks," Ruby replied. "It's almost like I'm craving fruits and veggies. I know, it's so strange." She saw the look of confusion on Opal's face and the look of horror on Maude's.

Ruby shrugged and paid for a small bag of figs and apples. The fruit seemed to settle her stomach instantly. She couldn't help but smile as Maude and Opal bought a couple dozen pastries each and were comparing them across a small table. She would probably sneak one later. It wasn't every day that a girl was in Rome eating true Italian pastries. Now to find a shop full of Roman goods. She was already redesigning her bedroom in her head.

"Okay, I'm fat and happy now. Where to?" Maude said leaning back away from the table.

"I want to see the Sistine Chapel," Ruby gushed. "And then time to shop!"

"I don't think we have time for all sixteen chapels, Ruby. You really need to pick one," Opal told her.

"Not sixteen. Sistine. Oh never mind. Let's go see what ol' Michelangelo is up to these days," Ruby smiled happily.

"Sorry," Opal said with a laugh. "I thought you were trying an Italian accent for a minute."

They made their way back to where the vespas were parked. "Anybody know how to get there?" Maude asked.

"I know the way!" Opal squealed. Before Maude and Ruby were fully on their vehicles, Opal was off and weaving into the traffic ahead.

"Where is she going?" Maude yelled at Ruby.

"I don't know. I've never been to Rome!" Ruby yelled back.

"Neither has she!" Maude reminded her.

They followed Opal as best they could, but they couldn't quite catch up to her. Much to their chagrin, Opal was having the time of her life zipping between cars going in every direction. Twice she darted off the main road onto smaller side streets. Maude was sure that Opal was going to get herself killed the way she was driving, but Opal didn't seem to have a care in the world despite the curses from the other drivers she cut off.

Luck must have been on Opal's side, because thirty minutes later she pulled up in front of a crowd of tourists at what turned out to be the Sistine Chapel. Ruby held her hand to her heart as they entered the chapel behind a long line of people.

"It's beautiful," Ruby exclaimed. She admired the beauty of the painting for a few minutes in silence.

"There's a lot of nekkid people," Opal commented.

"It's called art," Ruby corrected her.

"It wasn't called art when I said we should go to the nude beach," Opal said under her breath.

Art or not, Maude had to admit that Opal was right. "You would think he could have painted a few more clothes on some of them."

Ruby shook her head.

"Ok, where to next?" Opal asked.

"We just got here!" Ruby said aghast.

"Right, but now we've seen it and crossed it off the list. So, where to next?" Opal explained.

Maude agreed with Opal. The Chapel was beautiful, but there wasn't much to do aside from looking around. They weren't allowed to touch anything either, so after a few minutes of standing around, Maude was getting bored.

Ruby ignored them both and stayed transfixed on the spot. People were having to walk around her, but she didn't seem to mind.

"Earth to Ruby," Opal laughed. "Ready now?" Opal was getting antsier by the minute.

Ruby rolled her eyes and followed Maude and Opal outside to their vespas. "I haven't bought a single souvenir from Rome. Tomorrow's our last day here so I better load up this afternoon. Let's find some cute stores," Ruby said.

Maude was willing to go anywhere besides these stuffy old buildings that Ruby seemed to gravitate to. It did not take them long to find something that matched Ruby's expectations. Maude knew the moment they entered the first shop that her arms would be sore from lugging around all the shopping bags Ruby was about to load up.

Ruby spared no expense when it came to shopping. She had a knack for finding the beauty in everything she saw. There was not a knickknack in sight that Ruby didn't fall in love with. Within minutes in the first shop, Ruby found a stack of shirts, a green sundress, a floppy hat, a collection of Italian maps, and numerous figurines. Maude groaned when Ruby announced that the owner of the shop told her that his brother-in-law owned the shop across the street. She took that as a sign that she needed to peruse his inventory as well.

"Why the long face Maude?" Opal asked as they followed behind a skipping Ruby.

"How are we going to get all this junk back home?" Maude whispered.

"I'm sure we'll find a way," Opal laughed.

"Aren't you going to buy a couple of bags, too?" Maude asked.

"No need," Opal shrugged. "Ruby's already outfitted the both of us with a closet full of t-shirts. She doesn't realize half of what she buys anyway, so we'll end up with some of it, I'm sure."

Opal had a fair point. She followed behind Ruby into the next shop that was slightly bigger than the one they had just exited. The pastries had settled in Maude's stomach and she had to stifle a yawn. Ruby mistook her yawn for excitement and tossed her a statue of some ornate goddess and a small Italian flag.

"These are the cutest things I've ever seen!" Ruby squealed. Opal smiled softly and gently guided her to the checkout where Maude exhaled a sigh of relief. Ruby had only bought two bags of souvenirs in this store.

Their vespas were weighted down significantly as they made their way back to the hostel. They had planned to drop off their newly acquired things and change clothes before experiencing the Roman Coliseum in the center of the city later that evening.

"What exactly do you do at the Coliseum?" Maude asked.

"You fight gladiators, Maude," Opal said seriously.

"Oh stop," Ruby laughed. "You look around, take in the sights," Ruby shrugged. "It's history."

"Maybe that's what they want you to think," Opal said. "Then when you get there, bam! They throw you in front of a crowd of a couple thousand and you fight your way out!"

"You are seriously deranged," Maude said. She rolled her eyes at Ruby's sense of wanderlust and Opal's outright insanity. Maude knew the history of the Coliseum, but didn't understand Opal or Ruby's desire to see it. It would be different if there were actual soldiers and wild beasts still entertaining the crowds, but as far as she knew, it was just a shell of a building. Hopefully it was still safe to explore.

They decided to walk to the Coliseum since it was such a beautiful evening outside. Opal walked briskly ahead of Ruby and Maude pretending to slash imaginary passersby with her imaginary sword and shield. "I am the great Opal of the land Rhinestone. Beware all you saints and sinners alike," she giggled.

"She's crazy, you know that right?" Maude whispered to Ruby.

Ruby laughed and said, "She loves life, that's for sure. Sometimes I wish I could be free spirited and wild like she is, but then again maybe not."

Maude couldn't help but smile and nod in agreement. They continued to laugh at Opal's antics and followed her through the throngs of people who were also enjoying the good weather.

The Coliseum was bigger than any of them anticipated. The closer they got to it, the more in awe they were.

"Bring on the gladiators!" Opal cheered. She pounded on her chest and puffed herself up. A few people turned to stare at her, but Opal paid them no mind. "Come on, y'all!" she called back to Maude and Ruby.

Once again Ruby and Maude quickened their pace to keep up with Opal. They bought tickets for the last tour of the evening and gathered with a group of fellow tourists who were just as eager as they were.

They followed the group led by a young man who spoke broken English. They were only half listening as they walked carefully up the decaying steps. "Well this is nothing like the history books," Opal surmised as she looked around. "No bloody footprints, no shredded limbs from beasts. Hmm."

"It was thousands of years ago," Ruby laughed. "I hope there's no blood left around." Ruby shivered at the thought. It was getting darker outside and the evening air added to the ominous feeling the colossal building gave off.

"I want to see where the lions and tigers were kept," Opal whispered.

"No one's allowed down there," Ruby whispered back. "Thank God. I bet it's so creepy! Just thinking about it freaks me out!"

"I bet I could find it," Opal sneered.

"NO!" Ruby and Maude both shouted. Maude made sure to keep her eyes fixated on Opal who had a tendency to wander.

They could see the Roman Forum nearby as they scaled the upper balconies. "Let's go there tomorrow before we head to Naples," Maude said.

"Do you think we'll have time?" Ruby asked.

"Probably not," Maude sighed. "At least I can see it from here."

When they finished the tour, they walked over to a nearby food cart and purchased slices of pizza and gelato.

"I thought you said Italians don't eat pizza!" said Ruby sarcastically.

"You can't order pizza at a nice restaurant," said Opal. "But from a food cart on a nice evening like this, it's fine."

Ruby rolled her eyes at Opal's logic, but she enjoyed the excuse to eat pizza. It was the best pizza she had ever eaten and she considered herself to be a pizza aficionado.

"This ice cream is too good," Maude said dreamily.

"It's not ice cream," Opal hissed. "Shh, it's gelato!"

"Same thing," Maude replied.

"Au contraire," Opal said. "Not the same at all. It takes a refined palette to know the difference. I wouldn't expect you to know the difference."

"Let it go," Ruby winked at Maude. They continued to eat their gelato in the square. Someone brought out a guitar on a nearby balcony and someone else began to sing. Maude couldn't understand the words, but she could feel the emotion. She even laughed when Opal started to dance. It wasn't long before they were all dancing the evening away with friends and strangers alike.

By the time they got back to the hostel and packed their scattered belongings, they all fell straight into bed with smiles on their faces.

～Chapter Twenty～

Maude was the first to wake up the next morning. She shook Ruby and Opal till they too awoke. Surprisingly, Maude was also the first one dressed and packed. She waited impatiently for the other two to hurry up and get their things in order. She was more than ready to get to Naples. She could already visualize the beach where she was going to spend the next few days sunbathing.

"Come on, y'all. Naples is calling!" Maude said, finally shaking them awake.

"Okay, okay," Ruby moaned. She hadn't slept well. The pizza hadn't settled well on her stomach after all that dancing. She'd be glad to get back to Rhinestone away from all this rich food. It was too much for a country girl to take.

"Opal, get up," Maude continued to shake her shoulder.

"Give me twenty minutes and I'll be ready," Opal said, stretching her arms up to the heavens and she sat up in bed.

"You ain't never been ready in twenty minutes in your life!" Maude told her.

Opal shook her head at her friend. "Time works differently over here on this continent. Twenty minutes is longer here."

Maude and Ruby looked at her. "Time don't move differently in different parts of the world. Twenty minutes is twenty minutes!" Maude snapped at her.

"That just goes to show you don't have a continental mind," Opal sighed. She picked up her clothes and marched proudly towards the bathroom.

"I swear she gets crazier every day," Maude lamented.

"Yep. Just when we think she's reached her peak, she goes and surprises us all again," Ruby laughed.

"It'll be a miracle if I don't kill her one of these days," Maude said, shaking her head.

"You always say that, but admit it. You'd miss her if she wasn't around," Ruby winked at her.

"At this point, I'm willing to take my chances," Maude huffed.

Ruby folded her night clothes and stuffed as many of the souvenir bags into her luggage as she could.

"How in the world are we going to get all this stuff to the station?" Maude asked Ruby.

Ruby looked around. "Maybe I do need to buy another bag while we're in Naples. I may have bought a little more than I realized.

Maude looked around. A little? It looked like there were two dozen extra bags of souvenirs. She wasn't sure what else Ruby could buy that she hadn't already purchased. She quickly added as many things to her suitcase as she could, but that still left quite a few things straggling around.

"Aren't you finished packing yet? I'm ready to go," Opal said, waltzing in from the hallway.

"You should be ready. You left a half hour ago," Maude said.

"I told you time is different here," Opal brushed her aside.

Ruby shook her head at Maude. "Let it go," she whispered with a huge grin on her face.

"I'm so ready to go!" Maude said. "All the sun and sand, bring it on!"

"There's so much history in Naples," Ruby said. "It's close to Pompeii and Vesuvius. I bet there's a ton of markets we can visit!"

"I want to go cliff diving!" Opal whined.

"I'm sure we can find a cliff to push her off," Maude whispered to Ruby.

"I heard that," Opal winced.

"Only kidding!" Maude smiled. "Kinda."

"Positano is where the cliffs are," Niccolo smiled. He had peered around the open door of the room to say goodbye before heading off to his job. "It's been a pleasure meeting you ladies. Such true southern belles." He bowed and winked at Ruby who blushed.

"Ok, hear that? How do we get to Positano?" Opal asked.

"Don't even think we are going anywhere but Naples Italy, Opal Clementine!" Maude yelled.

"Shh! Don't use my government name," Opal hushed her. "No one knows me here like that."

"Do you think you're a secret agent or something? Nobody cares that your middle name is Clementine!" Maude smirked. She wrapped two of the bags with shoulder straps criss-crossed over her torso before picking up two more under each arm.

"Well, if we're using middle names then buckle up Maude," Opal started to say.

Maude clapped her hand over Opal's mouth before she could utter another word.

"Ouch!" Maude cried. "She bit me! Damn't Opal!"

Ruby had sank back down on the bed from laughing.

"Guess she sure showed you, Winifred," Ruby laughed.

"Not you, too, Ruby!" Maude said aghast.

It was Opal's turn to fall down laughing. "We must be a sight for sure," she gasped. "What drugs were our parents on when we were born!"

"There's nothing wrong with Winifred or Clementine," Ruby chuckled.

"Hush up, Ruby!" Maude scowled at her friends.

"Clementine is from that old cowboy song. How would you like to be named after a song?" Opal asked.

"I am," Ruby said.

"You are?" Maude asked. "Ruby or Morgan?"

"Yep. 'Icky Morgan Plays the Organ' by Glenn Miller. My parents loved him. It's a shame he died in the war," Ruby explained.

"That's great and all," Opal said. "But what I can't work out is where the heck Winifred came from?" Opal smiled wryly.

"From my mean and ugly old great-aunt Winifred who promised to leave her fortune to the first child to bear her name. Crazy old coot left me a pack of baseball cards and some ol' moldy letters and now I'm stuck with a name like Winifred," Maude grumbled.

"It's not so bad," Ruby smiled.

"It ain't so great," Maude said. "But it's better than my brother. His middle name's Muriel after her. She was Winifred Muriel. Can you imagine!"

"Maurice Muriel?" Ruby asked.

"Yes," she nodded.

"Bless his heart," Opal shook her head.

"They kinda set that poor kid up for life, didn't they?" Ruby said.

"Yeah, they did," Maude admitted.

"Well, when I have children I promise never to name them after dead great aunts!" Opal vowed.

"Me too!" Ruby laughed.

Maude chuckled as well. "It's a pact! Pinky swear."

They each interlocked their fingers and laughed at the absurdity of the agreement. Minutes later they were laughing their way toward the train station with Maude, as always, lugging the majority of the baggage. Opal skipped ahead to buy the tickets. Ruby stayed closer to Maude. She was hoping to find a chance to sneak into another shop before she left Rome.

Opal returned quickly with the tickets. She had also found some more gelato somewhere along the way.

"Where'd you get that?" Maude asked.

"Over there," she replied and pointed to a man pedaling a bicycle with a cooler attached to the back.

"I want some, too," Maude huffed. "Did you ever think of that?"

"Of course I did, Winnie," she winked. "Here!" She tossed her one and Maude had to drop one of the shopping bags to catch it.

"Don't start that again, Opal," Maude warned.

"I promise, that's the last time I'll bring it up," Opal smiled. "Ready? It's time to board."

Opal led the way to the platform and they filed onto the crowded train. Maude found seats at the far end of the car. By this time, they needed extra room for the souvenirs, which took up as much room as the three of them did.

They could feel the train gather speed as they left the station. Opal hung her head out the window and shouted, "Ciao Roma! Ciao!"

"Sit your butt down!" Maude ordered. "You could fall out that window and we'd have to explain to your mama and daddy how you got runned over by a train!"

"I ain't going to get run over by the train. You exaggerate so much sometimes, Maude," Opal said.

"Well, sit down anyway. The conductor is coming and he's looking at you like you're crazy," Maude said.

"Maybe he's never seen such a beautiful woman before," she said. Opal batted her eyes and did an awkward sort of dance as the conductor walked by.

"Yeah, that's got to be it," Maude said. Maude rolled her eyes and turned towards Opal. "He probably thinks we busted you out of some hospital. Can you behave for just one minute?"

"Of course I can. Can you?" Opal asked seriously.

"While you two squabble, I'm trying to figure out where exactly we go once we get off the train. I lost the paper where we wrote down the name of that hotel," Ruby admitted.

"That's ok," Opal assured her. "I have the mind of a steel trap."

"Oh it's a trap alright," Maude mumbled.

"It's called Vista Sull'Oceano," Opal said without paying Maude any attention.

"Oh that's really pretty," Ruby gushed.

"Yeah, I thought so. It means view of the ocean," Opal said proudly. "It sounds perfect."

"It must be right on the beach," Maude said. She hated to admit that Opal might have found the perfect place for them.

"I can't wait to get there," Ruby said. "Nothing is more relaxing than strolling along barefoot on the beach."

They began to chat about their upcoming adventures in Naples. Ruby was adamant they visit Pompeii and Vesuvius. Opal wanted to visit the underground tunnels and catacombs underneath the city. She also mentioned cliff diving every few minutes in case either Ruby or Maude forgot. Maude was ready to relax and spend all of her time soaking up the rays on the beach. She was getting giddy from excitement with each mile that passed. When they pulled into the station a few hours later, Maude scooped up as many bags as her arms could carry and left the rest for Ruby and Opal. She hopped off the platform and spun around. She was finally in Naples and nothing could drag her down.

"It looks like rain. Let's take a cab to the hotel," Ruby suggested.

"What? No it doesn't," Maude said.

The sky was getting grayer by the minute and they heard what was positively thunder in the background.

"Don't say it, Ruby. Don't speak it into being," Maude stomped her foot.

"It's fixing to rain whether you like it or not," Ruby shrugged.

Maude didn't like the idea of carrying their luggage all over the city, especially in a downpour, so she begrudgingly agreed. Opal gave a cat whistle which brought a taxi to them immediately.

"Dove stai andando?" the man asked. He got out of the car and began helping them load all their bags into the cab.

"To the beach. Opal, how do you say, beach?" Maude asked.

Opal recited the name of the hotel with an Italian accent heavily influenced by the deep South. She added, "tempo di spiaggia" with her hands raised in the air.

"Dove?" he asked again.

Opal repeated the information again.

"No, no," he waved her request off.

"Si, si" Opal was adamant.

He shook his head slightly, but drove off to the center of town.

"Is this the way to the beach?" Maude whispered to Ruby.

"I don't think so," Ruby said, looking out the window as one cramped building after another passed by.

The driver began ranting something in Italian that none of the girls could understand. He was speaking too fast for even Opal to catch on. He helped them unload their bags. Two men walked out of the hotel and began speaking loudly to the taxi driver. Ruby felt like she was in the middle of a very angry tennis match with each man yelling fiercely at the other.

"You sure? No good. You leave for new hotel?" he offered in broken English.

"You stay, yes?" The rounder of the two men asked.

"Um," Ruby stammered.

"Si, si. They stay," the younger man said. He picked up some of the bags before Maude could protest and headed into the lobby of the building.

"Um," Ruby stammered again.

"He just took our bags," Maude said, following the man inside.

By now the taxi driver was fully invested in the disagreement. He didn't seem to appreciate them walking away. He followed them inside where the argument reached new decibels. Minutes later, he was back outside shaking his head.

"Buona fortuna a te," the taxi driver shrugged. He got back into his taxi and peeled out of the parking lot.

Ruby and Opal went inside to find Maude who seemed to be holding her own against these two strange men.

"Those are my bags!" she yelled loudly.

"Si, si. You stay," the larger man said, this time much more politely.

"Opal, hold my earrings. I don't have time for this today!" Maude hissed. "I'm hungry, I'm tired, it's raining, and there ain't no beach for miles!"

"Si, si, you stay. You eat, you sleep, so good," he said again.

"I think there has been some mistake. We had reservations for a hotel with a view of the ocean. I don't think we're in the right place," Ruby offered as diplomatically as she dared.

"Si. Vista Sull'Oceano. Si," he nodded.

"No. No ocean. This is the city," Maude yelled slowly to help him understand her point. "This is false advertising!"

"Ah, si. Right there," he said. He pointed behind him to a large painting of an ocean. The corners were peeling and there were obvious stains on the frame, but the man was very excited as he eagerly pointed to the eyesore on the wall.

"Oh dear God in heaven! That's the view of the ocean we get?" Maude fumed.

"Vista Sull'Oceano," he smiled.

Maude glared at him

"Sei gli Americani?" he asked. He kept nodding his head and smiling.

"What?" Maude asked.

"Opal Tyler, Americans," he said. "You stay here. We have room, si."

Maude looked around to see the younger man already carrying their bags upstairs.

"This is crazy," Ruby whispered.

"The thing with crazy is, you gotta stay one step ahead of it. Like me. I let people think I'm crazy, but it's all an act." Opal explained

"Are you sure about this?" Ruby asked.

"I'm not so sure," Maude interrupted.

"Que sera sera," Opal shrugged. She followed the man up the stairs humming and dancing the entire way.

⚘Chapter Twenty-One⚘

"This isn't exactly what I had in mind when you said it had an ocean view," Maude huffed. This was supposed to be her grand adventure of a lifetime and nothing had gone right.

"I can't help they lie in Italian, too," Opal replied. "Might as well make the best of it."

Ruby agreed and rifled through her suitcase to find the new shirts she had found in Rome. "Here y'all, put these on," she said. Maude and Opal peeled off the shirts they were wearing and put on the new shirts. Now they all matched again.

"Where to first?" Opal asked.

"Uh, the beach. That's literally why we came to Naples. For the beach and the shirtless Italian men," Maude snapped. She sat down on the creaking bed and crossed her arms.

"We have plenty of time for the beach," Opal said soothingly. "Plus, it's raining. Let's go visit the underground catacombs while it's spooky outside!"

"I guess we can't go sunbathing while it rains. I'm game if you are, Maude," Ruby agreed.

"Oh alright," Maude said. "Let's get on with it then. The less we stay in this room the better." The walls were a putrid pink color and the paint was peeling near the borders. The beds creaked and the bathroom door did not lock. There was no balcony, nor any windows in the room at all. "I feel like the walls are closing in," Maude sighed.

"It could always be worse," Opal mused.

Maude glared at her. She didn't share Opal's optimism, but she didn't want to tempt fate either.

They exited the room and walked down the carpeted stairs to the front lobby. The men were still downstairs and watched them curiously as they left. Ruby had the sneaking suspicion that they were watching them to make sure they weren't taking their bags and running away to another hotel. No wonder Opal said she had gotten a great deal on this stay.

The sky was overcast, but the rain had slowed to a drizzle. Opal walked to a street sign on the corner and looked around for someone to ask. She found an elderly woman leaning on a walking stick and asked her the best way to the catacombs. From the grand hand gestures and laughter, Ruby could tell that they were not exactly close to their destination.

Opal hugged the woman and then beckoned Maude and Ruby to follow her as she cut through different side streets. After what felt like an hour of walking, they finally arrived at the Catacombs of San Gennaro.

"Come on, let's go," Opal said in excitement. "Ooooh, ahhhh, spooky spooky."

"Stop it, Opal! There's some things you don't mess with!" Maude snapped. "Get serious."

"Oh, I'm very serious. Serious about creeping you out!" Opal cackled.

"Cut it out, y'all," Ruby snapped. "People are staring."

Sure enough a few other tourists were staring awkwardly at them. "Nothing to see here," Maude said quickly.

"Just a field trip for the neighborhood lunatic," Opal laughed. "Don't worry, she's not as dangerous as she looks!" She grabbed Maude by the arm and led her to the entrance of the catacombs with Ruby following behind them laughing and shaking her head.

"Opal, stop," Ruby laughed.

"Come on Sister Ruby, let us begin the descent to the underworld," Opal cackled back. She looked around and realized that no one was following them. "Hmm, wonder why no one's coming with us. They must think you're really crazy, Maude."

Maude turned back to Ruby and rolled her eyes. "Help me," she mouthed.

They reached the stone slats that had been carved into the stone walls for centuries.

"Look! They have some openings!" Opal laughed. "Wanna boost, Maude? It's a sight nicer than our hotel room."

"After you," Maude said. She knew Opal was kidding, but the stone openings left her feeling slightly queasy. "It's cold down here." She wrapped her arms around herself and tried to rub the chills out of her body. She could feel Ruby shivering next to her.

"Doesn't smell so nice either," 'Ruby whispered to her.

"Well, yea, the smell of death never does," Maude replied.

"These look like little bunk beds," Opal pointed out. "I bet I can fit in this one."

"Don't you dare!" Ruby and Maude said together. They pulled Opal back by the arm and pushed her onward. The catacombs were dark and water dripped above their heads to the stone floor.

"No ma'am!" Ruby hissed at Opal who had tried to step over a rope barring anyone from crossing into the next tunnel. "There's a rope there keeping people back for a reason. You can't cross it!"

"I bet I could," Opal said under her breath. She sighed and walked between Ruby and Maude through the dimly lit tunnels. "What if someone just jumped right out of the walls?"

"Then they'd have a new body to replace it with because I'd die," Maude said. "Are we done here yet?"

"We just got here! Right Ruby?" Opal asked.

"I don't feel so good," Ruby said suddenly. Maude and Opal looked at her and noticed she looked pale and uneasy on her feet.

"Come on, let's get back to civilization," Maude said. She steered Ruby back to the stone steps as fast as she could. Opal hurried behind them and found a bench for them to sit down on.

"Are you ok?" they asked Ruby.

Ruby rubbed her eyes and slowly nodded her head. "I'm ok. It was just too much being down there. I think my feet need to stay on this level for awhile," she smiled.

"Maybe we should head back to the hotel. Just to be on the safe side," Maude said.

"No, no, I'm ok," Ruby said again. "I just needed some fresh air."

"Ok, can you walk? I think we need to head back to the hotel," Maude replied.

"I'm fine, I promise. We can walk around for a little while," Ruby said meekly. Maude helped her to her feet and together the three of them walked gingerly down the cobblestone street. The rain had all but stopped and the clean air seemed to do wonders for Ruby. They passed a gelato shop and Opal stopped in front of it.

"I think you need some fine Italian gelato,"' Opal said cheerfully.

"I think you're right," Ruby agreed.

Opal came out of the gelato shop a few minutes later with three cones. She licked one and handed the other two to Maude who recoiled when Opal dropped chocolate gelato onto her outstretched hand.

They sat underneath the umbrella outside the small gelato shop and enjoyed the noise of people walking by. Occasionally, Maude would glance over at Ruby who was still paler than normal. Ruby was only nibbling at her gelato and looked uncomfortable.

"Where to now?" Opal asked.

"I say Ruby needs to see a doctor," Maude said.

Opal turned to look at Ruby carefully. She could see Maude on Ruby's other side cutting her eyes at her. "I reckon Maude is right," Opal agreed.

"I don't need a fuss," Ruby said. "I'm fine. I just got a little winded and I haven't been sleeping well lately."

"You haven't been eating well either," Maude acknowledged.

"Maybe you have some rare old world disease that hasn't been seen in a few centuries," Opal said seriously. "We better find a local witch doctor."

"Thanks Opal. I haven't been too worried, but I am now," Ruby grimaced.

"Shut up Opal. Ruby, you don't have some crackpot disease that probably only exists in Opal's head. I'm sure it's nothing, but it wouldn't hurt to get a professional opinion," Maude said.

"I don't need a doctor," Ruby said with a hint of her old spirit. She took a deep breath and said. "Let's go explore some more.

They began walking down the long cobbled road toward one of the churches on the corner. It wasn't necessarily a tourist attraction, but there was an ancient cemetery beside it and Opal always

loved visiting cemeteries. She skipped ahead while
Maude stayed close to Ruby. Before Opal could
reach the gate of the burial ground, Maude was
calling to her.

"Opal! Opal! Get back here!" Maude shouted.

Opal turned around and saw Maude holding
Ruby up underneath her shoulder.

"What happened?" Opal asked, grabbing
Ruby's other arm.

"I just got so dizzy all of the sudden," Ruby
mumbled.

"You're going to a doctor!" Maude told her.

"Yeah, you need to see someone, Ruby," Opal
agreed.

"Alright," Ruby said begrudgingly. "If I go to
the doctor for y'all, can we just drop it and enjoy
our final days in Italy?"

"Yes," Maude and Opal agreed.

Several locals gathered around them after
seeing the pretty foreigner staggering with her two
friends. An older couple stepped up to help.

"Stai bene?" the man asked.

"Our friend needs a doctor," Maude tried to
gesture the word doctor to him.

"Medico," Opal said.

"Ah, medico," the man nodded.

"Yes, yes. Medico. A doctor, a real one, Opal,"
Maude said covering all possible languages.

"Si, si," he nodded again. He took Ruby's arm
away from Opal and gently guided her away from
the crowd. His wife linked arms with Opal and
followed her husband and Ruby up a small

alleyway toward another larger street conversing in rapid Italian.

"I don't like this," Maude mumbled as they made their way through the darkened alley.

"It's fine. Signora Rocci says the doctor is this way," Opal said to her.

"I still don't know where you learned this Italian," Maude hissed.

They took a left at the next street and walked about a half block to a small, simple door that had a red cross on the sign. The couple walked in and began an animated conversation with the receptionist.

Ruby sank into a small wooden chair by the door. She was feeling somewhat better, but she still looked a little peaked. Maude brought her a cup of water from the water cooler in the corner.

Opal explained that the doctor was the couple's son and he promised that he would take good care of their friend.

"Thank you," Ruby whispered.

"Grazie," Opal said.

A few minutes later, a stern looking nurse came out and escorted Ruby to the back. Maude stood up to go with her friend, but the nurse waved her away.

"She looks sweet," Opal whispered to Maude.

"Yeah. She's a real peach," Maude agreed. "Where are you going?" Maude called to Opal who was following Ruby and the nurse to the back.

"I'm her translator," Opal replied.

The nurse was less than pleased to have an audience following her back. She glared at Opal as she skipped lightly through the door to the back.

"No," the nurse grunted.

"Traduco," Opal smiled at her.

The nurse growled, but said nothing more.

Ruby was led to one of the three exam rooms where the nurse began checking Ruby's vitals. "Ogni possibilità che tu sia incinta?" the nurse hastily asked.

"No," Opal laughed. The nurse looked confused and gestured for Opal to ask Ruby, but Opal shook her head and smirked. "No, no," she laughed again.

The nurse shrugged and made some notes on her clipboard. "Il dottore arriverà presto," she said. She closed the door softly behind her.

"She said the doctor will be in soon," Opal said. "Hopefully he'll hurry up. It's boring in here." Opal walked over to the counter and opened the various jars. She pinched a cotton swab between her fingers and grabbed two tongue depressors and drummed on the sterile countertop.

There was a soft knock on the door and the doctor walked inside. He was refreshingly good looking and had a kind smile. "Ciao!"

"Hello there," Opal said. She introduced herself and Ruby to the handsome doctor and batted her eyes.

The doctor smiled and said, "I am Doctor Rocci. I speak a little English. You will help?" he motioned to Opal.

"I'm all yours, Doc," she crooned.

He pulled up a stool in front of Ruby and looked in her eyes, nose, ears, and throat. He felt her lymph nodes in her neck and pulled out his stethoscope. He breathed on the cool metal and instructed her to take a few deep breaths. "Ok, tell me what has gone on with you," he said to Ruby.

"She doesn't eat or sleep. She keeps getting dizzy and sneaks off to the bathroom to throw up a few times a day. She's not used to authentic cuisine, that's the problem," Opal interrupted.

Ruby shot her a look and rolled her eyes. "I'm fine, sir," she said.

"No," he said. "That's not fine." He grabbed the file from his lap and read over some notes from his nurse. " Qual è stata l'ultima data del tuo ciclo mestruale?"

"Um, I don't know," answered Opal. She looked confusedly at Ruby and back to the doctor.

"Ask her, per favore," he said.

"Um, he wants to know the last time Aunt Flo visited and I don't know. I'm good for another week and Maude is always on her it seems like, so what, it's been two weeks or so?" Opal asked.

Ruby fidgeted uncomfortably. "Um, I'm a little late," she whispered under her breath.

"What?" Opal said. "I can't hear you, Ruby."

"I'm a few weeks late," she whispered inaudibly again.

"How long late?" the doctor asked.

"Late?" Opal said. "Late for what? Ruby ain't' never been late a day in her life! You got it all wrong, Doc."

"Ummm, a few weeks," Ruby whispered and held three fingers to show the handsome doctor.

He nodded his head and ignored Opal's agape mouth next to him.

Ruby continued to count on her fingers. "Or maybe six weeks. Yeah, probably closer to six weeks now. Time really flies, doesn't it," she said quietly.

The doctor looked at Opal for clarification, but Opal had leaned against the back wall with her jaw hanging down to the floor. "Ruby!" Opal gasped.

"How you say, you ache?" he pointed to his stomach and his chest.

Ruby nodded and looked at the floor. She was deliberately ignoring Opal who had not yet recovered from the shock. The doctor stood up and opened the door. He called for the nurse and spoke rapid Italian to her outside the door. When he returned, he smiled gently and motioned for Opal to come closer and translate.

"Consultare un medico quando torni a casa. Andrà tutto bene," he said kindly.

"What did he say?" Ruby asked.

"Uh, he said see a doctor at home and everything is fine. I'm sorry, Ruby, but what?" Opal asked.

"Can you ask him if it's ok to go swimming and all that while we're still here?" Ruby asked.

Opal stared blankly at Ruby and ignored her question. "Ruby, did I hear him right? You're pregnant?"

"Si, incinta," the doctor repeated.

"What? I mean, how. No, no, don't tell me that. I mean, when? I need to sit down," Opal stuttered.

The doctor handed Opal a paper towel and looked back at Ruby. "Congratulazioni," he smiled. The nurse entered the room and handed Ruby two cups of water and motioned for her to drink them.

Opal groaned and the doctor asked, "Qualsiasi altra cosa ti serva?"

Ruby looked at Opal who shook her head. "No, no, you've said enough," she gulped.

The doctor smiled again and exited the room leaving the two women alone in the silence.

"Opal? Please don't tell Maude. Not yet anyway. I want to tell her. I just don't know how yet," Ruby whispered.

"Well, you're taking this well!" Opal said.

"I kinda had an inkling," Ruby admitted. "Just promise to keep this a secret for now."

Opal's eyes bugged out of her head. "Ok, I won't tell Maude. She's not as worldly and modern as I am." Opal took two deep breaths and tried to steady herself before standing up. She grabbed one of the cups from Ruby and downed the water.

There was a sharp knock on the door and for a minute they thought the doctor was coming back in.

"Y'all ready?" Maude asked briskly. "That cute doctor said y'all were done and we could go. You okay, Ruby? I've been waiting, but what's the hold up? What'd he say?"

Ruby shot Opal a look and answered, "He said everything is fine and not to worry. And um, that was about it. I probably just ate some rotten food or something." She could hear Opal let out an exasperated sigh behind her.

"What's wrong with her?" Maude pointed to Opal.

"I don't remember you swallowing a baby," Opal mumbled.

"I beg your pardon," Maude stared at Ruby.

"Hush," Ruby hissed. Opal shrugged and replied, "I'm just saying."

"I don't think I heard correctly," Maude said after a few seconds.

"Yea, I thought the same thing at first," Opal said.

"Will someone explain to me what exactly is going on?" Maude demanded.

"Oh Maude. Probably should have had this talk with you a long time ago. You see, when two people love each other they," Opal started.

"Stop!" Ruby tried to smile. "Ok," she took a deep breath and braced herself to deliver the news. "I'm having a baby," Ruby admitted before the tears began to trickle down her cheeks.

"We're having a baby," Opal corrected her. "Well, not we as in you and me, but she gets the picture, I'm sure."

Maude looked just as stunned as Opal had been when she first heard the news. "Since when? Who? Is it? Nope, not going there," Maude stuttered.

"See? I knew she'd take it this way," Opal said to Ruby. "You should have prepared her better."

"I didn't plan to tell anyone like this! I wasn't altogether sure of anything, to tell you the truth, but that's neither here nor there now. And you know as well as I do whose it is," Ruby said.

"Well damn! But Opal's right. We're all in this together. We're having a baby and we're going to make sure that little munchkin has everything she can ever want!" Maude cheered.

"We don't know that it's a girl. But either way, I'm going to be the best aunt ever!" Opal said enthusiastically. "You can be second best, Maude."

"Oh dear God. Somebody save that poor child!" Maude shook her head.

Despite the news, Ruby found herself laughing at the thought of what Opal and Maude would teach her child.

"How many weeks or did he say?" Maude asked.

"Well, he didn't go into a lot of those details. He said we needed to see a doctor once we got home," Opal answered. "But according to my calculations, she's got to be at least two weeks, because that's how long we've been traveling."

"Wait a minute," Maude interrupted, "She broke up with him two weeks before that."

"Oh that's right, so it's at least a month, but they've been together for six years, so who knows how far along she could be," Opal shrugged.

Maude caught her breath and looked at Ruby with big eyes. "Ruby Morgan," she stated.

"Ok, now that you two have caught up on your math lessons, let's get out of here. There's a beach calling our name somewhere!" Ruby smiled. She wiped her eyes with the tissue Maude held out to her and stood up to leave.

"Don't think you're going to get off the hook that fast," Maude admonished her. "You've got loads to tell us and we've got all the time in the world." She held the door open for her two friends and followed them to the counter for Ruby to check out.

Chapter Twenty-Two

"I still can't believe it," Maude whispered to Opal. Ruby was back in the bathroom which gave them time to talk.

"Who you telling?" Opal replied. "I near about fell out when the doctor suggested it. Shh, she's coming back."

Maude continued to get dressed and Opal decided to do her morning stretches. They had a big day ahead of them and no time to dilly dally.

"Stop whispering. I'm pregnant, not deaf," Ruby said. She couldn't help but laugh at the guilty looks on her two friends' faces.

"Sorry, Ruby. It's just so crazy," Opal explained.

"I know," Ruby agreed. "No one knows that better than me. Now I answered all your juicy questions last night, so, let's get going this morning! I've always wanted to see Pompeii!"

"All I'm looking forward to is cliff diving this afternoon!" Opal squealed. "You have an excuse not to dive, Ruby, but you don't Maude. Unless there's something you need to tell us?"

"I'm telling you right now, I'm pushing her off the first cliff I see," Maude whispered to Ruby.

"Make sure you stretch before we leave," Opal warned. She stood up straight and reached her arms high above her. "I'll teach you the proper form, Maude. Here, watch." Opal leaned forward and dove across the bed.

Maude threw a pillow at her and told her to hurry up. They had to walk back to the train station to catch the next train. Maude was not excited about their train ride to Pompeii. Thankfully it only took about thirty minutes which allowed just enough time to admire the scenery, but not enough to go stir crazy. They walked the short distance to the entrance of the famous ruins.

"Oh look, the next tour starts in fifteen minutes," Ruby said as she read the information pamphlet.

"A two hour guided tour of the most famous structures and archeological finds throughout the famous city of Pompeii," Opal read aloud over her shoulder.

"Two hours, huh? You sure you're up to that Ruby?" Maude asked in an overly motherly sort of way.

"Of course I am. I didn't come all this way to miss Pompeii," Ruby said.

"Well, Mama has spoken. We're taking the tour!" Opal said. Before Maude could say another word, Opal marched up to the counter and bought the tickets for the three of them. There wasn't anyone else around besides the three of them.

"Kinda dead around here, am I right?"'Opal said.

"Too soon, Opal," Maude said, cringing. "You never know when it could happen again."

"It's been two thousand years, Maude. I think we're safe," Opal replied.

"With you around, there ain't nothing safe," Maude mumbled.

"Y'all behave. I think this is our tour guide. We don't want him to think we're crazy," Ruby said, motioning to a distinguished looking Italian man.

"Give him a few minutes and he'll know that we are," Opal sang happily.

"Hush up," Ruby whispered.

"Buongiorno e benvenuto," the tour guide said. "Mi chiamo Carlo, e tu sei?"

"Hi," Maude waved shyly.

"Hello," Ruby offered.

"Buongiorno Carlo. Mi chiamo Opal e i miei amici Maude e Ruby," Opal said. Carlo smiled and Opal pointed to Ruby and Maude and added, "Americans."

"Americani. Si, si," Carlo smiled. "You speak Italian very well," he told Opal.

Opal smiled smugly over at Maude who shot her a questioning look.

"But I speak English a little for your friends, yes," Carlo smiled at Ruby and Maude.

"Thank you," Ruby said politely.

Carlo began the tour by giving the ladies a detailed history of the disaster and the devastation that occurred in the first century. Ruby hung onto every word that he said. Maude kept a watchful eye on Opal, while also making sure that Ruby didn't get too winded.

"I'm fine, Maude," hissed Ruby. She could feel Maude's eyes boring a hole into the side of her face.

Maude nodded, but refrained from further comment. She turned her head just in time to catch Opal trying to open a gate barring entrance to visitors.

"Opal! What are you doing? You can't go in there!" Maude called after her.

"This has to be where they keep the good stuff," Opal said innocently.

Carlo came over to where Opal and Maude were standing. "No, no. Not safe!" he yelled.

Opal glared at Maude who stared right back at her. "You got me in trouble," Opal fumed.

"I kept you from breaking your neck," Maude countered.

"Will y'all two behave! I'm trying to learn about Pompeii," Ruby hissed at them once Carlo had gone back to his tour.

"I'm going to get you for this," Opal whispered to Maude. "I've been keeping score."

"Don't you threaten me, Clementine!" Maude warned her.

Ruby gave them both a stern look to quiet the commotion. Maude gave Opal a not-so-gentle push to move her closer to Ruby and Carlo. Thankfully,

Ruby missed this and Maude was able to give her an innocent look when she looked back.

"Opal, you stop acting up. I mean it," Ruby hissed at Opal again.

For the next hour and a half, they all listened intently as Carlo described the different discoveries. By the time they made it to the gift shop, Opal and Maude seemed to have put the feud behind them. At least, they weren't bickering like children anymore. To Ruby's relief, they were actually joking with each other as they often did.

"I think I got some good pictures," Ruby said. They were walking back to the train station and Maude interrupted, "I hope so! You had us pose enough times."

The train ride to Positano took an hour and a half. Maude and Ruby both nodded off a few times, but Opal was wide awake with excitement. She could barely sit still. She pulled her feather boa out of her bag and wrapped it around her neck. When the train pulled into the station, she made sure they were the first ones off the train.

"Here we are! Here we are!" Opal cheered. "I can't believe I'm going to actually go cliff diving! Come on y'all!" Opal took off in the direction of the large cliffs that looked in the background.

"Come on Maude, we did promise," Ruby said.

"I'd rather have all my teeth pulled than jump off a perfectly good cliff," Maude said. "At least you have an excuse, Ruby."

Ruby knew Maude wasn't looking forward to this at all. They followed after Opal who had already charged ahead at a quick pace. Positano was the perfect Italian village for cliff diving. There were multiple cliffs to choose from and the walkways between them were perfect for the crowded tourists to walk along. Opal headed for the tallest one, but Ruby cautioned her about starting small.

"You only live once, Ruby! We'll meet you back at the bottom. Come on Maude!" Opal said excitedly.

"I'm not jumping, Opal. I'll come with you to make sure you don't kill yourself on the way up, but then I'm climbing right back down,"'Maude replied.

"We'll see about that," Opal said under her breath.

Ruby watched the two of them head off to one of the medium cliffs. She sat down on the beach near the water's edge to wait for them. It was fun watching all of the locals and tourists alike jump from the cliffs into the warm water.

Suddenly she heard a commotion from the top of one of the cliffs and saw a figure fly into the water screaming the entire way. Another figure dove into the air and gracefully landed in the water not far from the first figure. Ruby recognized Opal's boa instantly.

Ruby stood up and cupped her hands around her eyes to get a better look. She saw Opal emerge from the water and shake her hair.

"That was such a rush! Oh my God, Ruby! We'll have to come back when you're, well, you know," Opal said. "Come on Maude!"

Maude emerged from the water next looking as wild as ever. She was fuming. "I'm going to kill you! I mean it this time! I'm going to do it!"

"I thought you weren't going to dive, Maude?" Ruby said. It took a bit of effort to hold Maude back.

"Ask her," Maude sneered. She pointed to Opal and coughed up more water from her lungs.

"She just needed a little convincing," Opal shrugged. "You wouldn't have choked if you had kept your mouth shut. There was no need to scream like that."

"Oh dear God! You could have killed her," Ruby said.

"The guy up there said no one has died in at least a year. It's perfectly safe. I just gave her a gentle push," Opal said.

Maude lunged for Opal, "Gentle push? You ran up and shoved me while I was looking over the edge! I really am going to kill you!"

Ruby braced herself between the two. "Maude, take it easy. You don't want to end up in an Italian prison."

"Yeah, those outfits will not flatter that figure of yours," Opal said earnestly.

Ruby turned on Opal instantly, "Opal! Behave!"

Opal stuck out her lip like a scolded child, but at least she was quiet for the moment.

"Now, let's find somewhere to eat," Ruby suggested.

"We passed a place with a great view up on the cliff. Just don't get too close or Opal will push you off." Maude offered.

Before Opal could respond, Ruby was separating them again. "Sounds good to me. Let's go," she added quickly.

The view was breathtaking. The walls were made of a thin glass that allowed the reflection of the sun coming off the water to permeate the restaurant. Ruby ordered a pasta dish with tomatoes that tasted better than anything she had ever eaten. Maude settled for a salad in hopes that it would settle her unsteady stomach. Her fifty foot fall into the warm water had jarred her completely. She picked at the salad and took a few more deep breaths while Opal plowed away at her chicken dish.

"I can't believe tomorrow is our last full day here," Ruby said.

"And we still haven't had a day at the beach," Maude said as she sipped her wine.

"You went swimming today. Isn't that close enough?" Opal asked with her mouth full of chicken.

Maude's face turned red and she gritted her teeth to keep from telling Opal just how deep she'd bury her if she had the opportunity.

"I think Maude is right. A nice relaxing day at the beach would be the perfect end to this adventure," Ruby offered diplomatically.

"Well, it won't be as fun as the swim we already had today, but I guess if Maude insists," Opal said and shrugged her shoulders.

Maude quickly finished her glass of wine and called for another one.

Ruby decided to change the subject to something less likely to cause Maude to murder Opal. "We still need to stop by a gift shop and get a few last souvenirs. We won't have another chance before we leave."

"I haven't seen any gift shops around here," Opal said.

"How could you see any gift shops when you were so busy trying to kill me," Maude huffed.

"Don't forget that we're flying out from Rome. You'll have plenty of time to snag something there if you really need to," Opal reminded her.

Ruby was so busy laughing at them she couldn't eat her pasta.

"What's so funny?" Maude asked.

"You two. We've gone around the world and the only thing you've both accomplished is you didn't kill each other, but God help you if the day comes when I'm not around to babysit you two. Y'all will never survive!" Ruby laughed.

"Maude's life would be boring without me," Opal grinned.

"I don't think you'll ever let me be bored!" Maude lifted her glass of wine to her friends.

They spent the rest of the meal laughing loudly at the adventures they'd had over the past two weeks.

"No one at home will believe half of these stories," Ruby said, rubbing her eyes.

"Yeah, they will. You've bought half of every city we've visited," Maude said.

"Plus we've got pictures," Opal said. "It's really too bad you didn't have one of those home movie recorders, Ruby. Everybody would have loved to have seen Maude's face when she jumped from the cliff."

"Pushed! I was pushed. Let's not forget you tried to kill me," Maude shot back at Opal.

"Don't worry Maude. If I was trying to kill you, you'd really be dead," Opal countered.

"Really be dead? How can you really be dead?" Ruby asked.

"It's easy enough to understand really. It's the opposite of being really alive," Opal explained to them as though it were the simplest concept imaginable.

"Like you've been telling me this whole trip, don't argue with her. Just let it go," Maude said. The wine was obviously having its desired effect.

They caught the bus to take them back to the train station. It was dark when they returned to Naples and began strolling up the street toward their hotel.

⌒Chapter Twenty-Three⌒

"The sun's not even up yet," Opal whined.

Maude was already dressed. Ruby turned over and pulled the blanket over her head. "I'm with Opal. It's too early to get up," Ruby whimpered.

"I waited this entire trip to spend some time on the beach. It's not raining, we aren't getting shoved off cliffs today, nor do we have any volcanoes to learn about. I'm going to the beach with or without y'all," Maude said sternly. She pulled her hat down over her eyes, grabbed her oversized bag, and marched out the door.

"Well that was dramatic," Opal laughed.

"I guess we better go after her," Ruby said, pushing the covers off.

"Oh, alright," Opal said with an exasperated sigh. She jumped off her bed and threw open the door. "Maude wait! We'll be right down! Maude? We'll be down soon!" she screamed down the hallway. "I don't know if she heard me or not," Opal said as she came back into the room.

"I think people in the next town over heard you," Ruby said. She rubbed her ears that were ringing from the shrillness of Opal's high pitched yell.

Maude was standing by the front desk when Ruby and Opal came down the stairs fifteen minutes later.

"Took you long enough," Maude hissed. The two owners of the hotel were in another heated discussion. Maude seemed greatly relieved to see her friends coming to her rescue.

"I thought you two wouldn't ever get down here. I thought they were going to come to blows," Maude told them once they were safely outside in the fresh air.

"What were they arguing about?" Ruby asked.

"I don't know. I heard one of them say something about spaghetti, but that was all I could make out," Maude said shaking her head.

"Spaghetti? I don't know why people get so upset about trivial things like that. Not everyone can remain as cool and calm as we do under pressure," Opal replied without the first hint of sarcasm.

Ruby and Maude both stared at her. Then they burst out in laughter.

"What?" Opal asked.

"Nothing," Ruby said, wiping a tear from her eye.

"We're just being cool and calm under pressure," Maude assured her and laughed even harder.

"Sometimes I think y'all are touched in the head," Opal said, not finding the slightest bit of humor in this conversation. "If I wasn't here to lead this group sometimes, I don't know where y'all would end up."

"Yea, probably somewhere like Nepal," Ruby whispered to Maude. Ruby and Maude were in such a fit of giggles by the time they walked to the bus stop that they almost missed the bus heading to the beach.

The trio drew quite a few concerned looks from the other passengers, but they didn't mind. This was the last full day of their vacation and they were determined to enjoy every minute of it.

"Smell that salt air," Maude said. She unrolled her beach towel and plopped down on it.

"Did you bring any snacks?" Opal asked. "You got us up so early that we didn't get breakfast."

"I knew I forgot something," Maude sniffed.

"How about I walk down the beach and see if anyone is open yet? I'll bring some food back and you hold our spot," Opal suggested.

"I'll go with you, Opal. I want to see if there's any shells," Ruby said.

"You just want to find a little seaside shop," Maude laughed. "But that's fine. I'll hold down the fort here and y'all go have some fun."

Opal and Ruby laid down their towels on either side of Maude and grabbed their bags.

"Sure you'll be ok here?" Opal asked.

Maude peered over the lens of her sunglasses and assured them that she would be fine. Ruby shrugged and linked arms with Opal as they turned to walk down the beach.

"Hopefully she won't get kidnapped while we're gone," Opal said.

"They'd bring her back. Trust me," Ruby laughed.

"Now about that breakfast," Opal said looking around. The beach was very quiet so early in the morning. The sun was beginning to appear behind some clouds and people were slowly making their way to the water's edge.

"I see a fruit stand ahead," Ruby pointed out.

"Thank the Lord. I'm about to pass out," Opal yawned.

They walked closer to the stand and Ruby's eyes lit up when she saw that the vendor also had shirts hanging in the front of the stand. Opal laughed while Ruby piled her arms full of shirts and seashell necklaces. She held up a shirt small enough for a toddler and Opal nodded. "That's adorable," she agreed.

They grabbed their bags full of souvenirs, fruit, and breakfast pastries and headed back to where they had left Maude.

"Are you sure this is the right way?" Ruby asked Opal.

"Oh, I was following you," Opal shrugged. She bit into a crisp apple and looked around.

"I think we might be lost," Ruby acknowledged.

"Well, I'm not sure asking anyone for directions would help either. I don't remember where exactly we left Maude," Opal giggled.

Ruby took a deep breath and thought hard. "The water was on our right when we left, so to head back, we should make sure the water is on our left. Right?" Ruby asked.

"Right it should be on our left or right it should be on our right?" Opal replied.

"I don't even know anymore honestly," Ruby giggled. "Let's turn around and walk the other way and see if any of it looks familiar."

The morning sun was beaming down on the sunbathers when Opal and Ruby returned some time later. Maude was lying on her stomach on the oversized towel. Their things were still piled exactly where they were left.

"Is she alive?" Opal wondered.

"I think she's asleep," Ruby said, studying Maude more closely.

"We should probably wake her up and tell her to roll over. It looks like she's done on that side," Opal said.

"She is a bit pink, isn't she?" Ruby agreed.

"Pink? That's the reddest shade of pink I've ever seen," Opal said.

Ruby touched Maude's shoulder and tried to gently nudge her. "Maude, it's time to wake up. I think you drifted off to sleep," Ruby said.

"And burned yourself to a real crisp," Opal added.

"Huh, what? Are y'all back already?" Maude asked.

"We've been gone for a good little while. You might want to turn over. You've got enough sun on your back," Ruby suggested.

"You're looking a little like my brother's pig, Bacon, when he became, well, bacon," Opal offered.

"Shh," Ruby whispered.

"Yeah, I must have dozed off for a few minutes. It's so relaxing here," Maude said, rolling over on her back. "Ooh, it feels like I got a little too much sun on my back."

"I'll say. You look like a lobster back there," Opal said.

"Stop comparing our friend to animals!" Ruby warned her.

"Did I get burned really bad?" Maude asked Ruby.

"Well, you got plenty of sun," Ruby offered kindly.

"I've seen fire trucks that weren't that red," Opal added.

Maude ignored Opal. She focused her attention on Ruby. "It kinda stings a little" she admitted.

"I mean, if you were a steak, I'd send you back to the kitchen for being raw," Opal reiterated.

"Oh God, is it that bad?" Maude asked Ruby.

Ruby did not want to scare her, so she gave her head a little twitch and encouraged Maude to turn over.

"Probably shouldn't fall asleep this time," Opal said. Ruby had to agree.

"Sure you don't want to come wade in the water with us or something? Get you up and moving," Opal asked.

"No, y'all go ahead. I'm going to enjoy every second out here I can," Maude said.

"Might get more than you bargained for," Opal said quietly.

"Come on, Opal, let's give Maude some quiet time," Ruby offered. They left Maude laying on her back. They walked to the water's edge and marveled at the beautiful water.

"What if there's a shark or, I don't know, whatever's worse than a shark?" Ruby asked.

"The odds of a shark getting us after all we've been through is astronomically low," Opal laughed. "I just want to put my feet in anyway."

Ruby followed her into the water and looked at all of the people who were congregating on the beach. It had sure filled up since they first arrived hours ago.

"Is there anything else you want to do while we're here?" Opal suddenly asked.

Ruby thought hard and shook her head. "Not really. I can't think of a single thing that is pressing. When we set off on this adventure, there was so much I wanted to do and see. But now I just want to enjoy the time we have left here and soak up the memories."

"It's been amazing, hasn't it?" Opal said.

"It really has. We'll never have another adventure as wild as this," Ruby said.

"I don't know, Ruby. You're going to be a mother. That's the ultimate adventure of a lifetime," Opal smiled.

"I'm glad I have you two along for the ride," Ruby agreed. They sat down at the water's edge and let the gentle waves rush over them. The sun was warm and felt good on their backs.

"It's starting to heat up," Opal said. "I could go for some gelato in this weather."

Ruby nodded and stood up to stretch. "I could go for gelato. I could go for lunch, too. It's about that time. You know it really is getting warm out here," she agreed.

All of a sudden both women looked at each other and shrieked, "Maude!" They hurried back over to Maude who was sound asleep on her back. The people who had been laying next to her had given her a wide berth due to her outrageous snoring. She was a brutal shade of crimson across her exposed legs, arms, and neck.

"Give me a stick or something to poke her," Opal said.

"We can't poke her! I don't have a stick anyway," Ruby muttered. "Hey Maude, time to wake up."

Maude yawned and stretched her arms above her head. "Ow," she mumbled. "I think I slept wrong or something."

"Oh, it's all kinds of wrong alright," Opal said. "Come on, let me help you get up."

Maude accepted Opal's outstretched hands and let Opal pull her up. "Ooh, I've been laying down too long. I feel so stiff," she whined.

"Um, are you going to tell her or should I?" Opal said to Ruby.

"Maude, you're pretty sunburned," Ruby said gently.

"I don't think that's the correct term, Ruby. Maude, you're sun broiled," Opal countered.

"How is that possible?" she asked. "I only took a cat nap."

"How many cats are you counting, Maude? You've been asleep for hours," Opal explained.

Maude looked around at the populated beach and shook her head. She removed her sunglasses and Ruby gasped. "What? What's wrong?" Maude asked.

"I'd put those back on if I were you," Opal chuckled.

"What Ruby?" Maude asked loudly. She was getting impatient.

"Um, it appears that your sunglasses did their job," Ruby said kindly. "They protected your eyes, but um, you've got an outline now. Um, your face under the glasses is fine, normal, but the rest of you is not."

"Oh dear God," Maude said. "Is it really that bad?"

Opal rummaged through her bag and found her compact mirror. "It ain't great," she said. "Here, take a look for yourself."

Maude sighed heavily and handed Opal her mirror back. "I'm going to rinse off in the water and then figure out what to do." She started to the water and left Opal and Ruby to confer.

"She can't exactly wash it off," Opal said.

"She knows that. I think she just meant rinse off the sweat and maybe splash some water on her. I don't know," Ruby replied honestly.

"OW!" Maude screeched.

Ruby and Opal rushed towards Maude who was exiting the water. "Something bit me!" she squealed.

"What? Where?" Ruby yelled.

"On my leg! Right there!" Maude said. She sank down into the sand and held her leg. There was a large red print on the back of her calf.

"That's a jellyfish," Opal whistled. "It got you good!"

"It burns!" Maude howled. "Help me!" A crowd had gathered around her and people were pointing.

"What should we do?" Ruby asked.

"Everybody knows you have to pee on a jellyfish sting. Don't worry, I got you, Maude!" Opal yelled. "Hey you, good looking fella, come over here for a second."

"Opal, what are you doing?" Ruby asked.

"Don't worry, I'm going to take care of Maude," Opal assured her.

"What are you doing?" Maude asked.

"Hey, Signor. Can you help my friend? She needs you to pee on her," Opal asked as though it was the most natural thing in the world to ask a complete stranger. "Medusa."

"OPAL!!" Maude yelled. "Don't call me that!"

"What? That's a medusa," Opal explained.

"I'll show you Medusa, you ape!" Maude howled.

"Opal, that's rude!" Ruby squealed.

"No, medusa!" Opal pointed to Maude. "It means jellyfish. Ugh, y'all are the reason they think Americans are dumb." She was beyond exasperated. "He pees on the medusa and the sting goes away. Simple as that!"

"Opal! Oh my Lord, you did not just ask him that!" Ruby said. "No one will be peeing on Medusa or anyone today!"

"Sorry amici, she says she'd rather suffer," Opal shrugged. The man walked away looking dejected.

"Let's just go back to the room! This has been the worst!" Maude howled.

Ruby told Opal to go gather up all their things. She stayed with Maude to make sure the Italian gentleman didn't return to render any first aid.

"We're going to need to find you some lotion or something. Otherwise it's going to be a long ride home," Ruby said.

"Oh, I don't even want to think about it," Maude mumbled.

"I've got the bags. Maude, your towel is covered in sand. Sorry about that," Opal said.

"Don't take a picture now!" Maude wailed. "Let's go back to the room."

Opal shoved the camera back into the bag and followed behind Maude and Ruby.

~ Chapter Twenty-Four ~

Their last evening in Italy proved less eventful than all their previous days. Ruby and Opal spent the evening packing and listening to Maude complain about her sunburn and sting. Ruby snuck out for an hour to purchase some more luggage. She would never tell Maude that she may have gone overboard buying souvenirs. She found two nice leather suitcases on wheels and showed them off proudly to Opal once she returned.

"Glad you're back! Maude is having trouble getting comfortable," Opal explained.

"I got you some more aloe while I was out," Ruby said gently.

"Thanks. I can't believe this happened," Maude scowled.

"You're the one who fell asleep," Opal told her.

"Don't remind me," Maude groaned.

"Want me to rub some more lotion on your shoulders?" Ruby asked.

"Yes, please," Maude admitted.

"She's going to need another bottle of lotion at the rate we're going," Opal said.

"We can get some more tomorrow morning before we get to the airport," Ruby assured her.

No one slept well that night. Maude moaned and complained with the slightest movement. Opal didn't know which was worse, Maude's snoring or her complaining. Ruby said nothing about their bickering. Her thoughts were filled with thoughts of the baby and the conversations she knew were coming over the next few days.

The sunlight shining through the gap in the curtains woke Ruby up the next morning. She stretched her hands over her head casually. She glanced at her watch and saw that it was a quarter past nine.

"Oh my goodness! We overslept!" Ruby screamed.

"Huh," Opal shrugged from within the blanket ball she had created.

Maude groaned in response.

"Come on you two. We've got to get to the train," Ruby said and she roughly shook them both.

"Ow!" Maude yelled.

"Our flight's not till threeish," Opal reminded her.

"Threeish isn't a time," Ruby retorted. "It's half past three. I checked."

"Come on Maude," Opal yawned. "You know how she gets when she's all riled up about something. Ugh." She slapped Maude playfully, but hard, on the shoulder to get her attention.

"Owww!" Maude sat up quickly.

"Oh, sorry Maude. I forgot," Opal said. "Well at least you're up now."

"Come on, y'all. We have to get to the train station and then bus over to the airport. Oh, we're never going to make it on time!" Ruby wailed.

"Yes, we will," Maude said. "Opal, go downstairs and check out of this place and we'll meet you downstairs."

Opal threw some things in her bag and tossed her pillow over her shoulder. "Ok, shouldn't take me long," she said.

"You sure that's a good idea?" Ruby asked.

"We all know I'm going to end up with the bags anyway," Maude huffed.

Opal took the carpeted stairs two at a time and landed gracefully in the lobby in front of the counter. The two men were sitting behind the counter with their arms crossed.

"Si sono divertiti perché non hanno dovuto ascoltarti!" Luca, the younger man said in a not so hushed whisper.

"Non parlarmi così, idiota. Potresti imparare molto ascoltandomi!" Bartolo retorted.

"Cosa posso imparare da te quando non puoi nemmeno far bollire l'acqua?" Luca replied.

"Signorina, digli che il segreto di un'ottima salsa è sempre l'origano. È troppo stupido per capire queste cose," Bartolo implored Opal.

"Lei non lo sa!" Luca laughed.

Opal thought about this for a moment. "L'origano è molto buono ma hai bisogno anche di basilico e aglio," she offered sagely.

"Sì!" Bartolo said. "L'americano lo sa!"

"No! She agrees with me!" Luca interjected.

"No! No!" Bartolo argued.

"Actually, it's a matter of personal taste. Mia madre says everyone has their own personal style. I'm not big on oregano actually, but," Opal started to say.

"Origano? L'origano è il migliore!" Bartolo yelled.

"See! Even the American knows you need more than oregano in good cooking!" Luca yelled.

"Even the American?" Opal asked.

"You young people! All alike no matter where you're from!" Bartolo threw his hands in the air in frustration.

"Americans know how to cook too, you know," Opal added. "Rosmarino, very fine." Opal was already getting heated listening to this gentleman belittle his young counterpart, but for him to start in on her too was just too much. She had been planning on helping Luca win the argument, but at this point she thought they were both being rude.

"Admit it! You're mad that an American is a better cook than you," Luca laughed at Bartolo.

Bartolo spit at the floor again and slammed his fist on the counter. "Gli americani non sanno cucinare!"

"Now wait just a minute here," Opal said, louder this time to try to be heard over the two yelling men. "What did you say about all Americans?"

"Odora di porcile!" Bartolo shouted. "Peggio degli americani!"

"Well, that's just rude," Opal said.

"Cosa intendi?" Luca asked aghast.

"Di porcile!" Bartolo spit on the floor. "Anche tu!"

"Why I never!" Opal gasped.

"Tua madre è un cavallo!" Luca shouted.

"Tua madre!" Bartolo shouted.

"My mother?" Opal asked.

"Sta 'zitto!" Luca shouted at Opal.

"I'm just here to check out," Opal yelled.

Bartolo sighed and held up his hand to Luca to pause their conversation. "Attendere prego." He looked back at Opal. "Ti è piaciuta la vista?" he asked her gruffly. "Very nice, no?"

"Well, now that you mention it," Opal said. "There's no view at all."

Bartolo and Luca glared at her.

"Senza vista," Opal clarified. "Brutta vision."

Bartolo's face reddened suddenly. "What wrong with view?"

"Mi hai mentito," Opal said. "You lied. Senza vista."

Bartolo turned to Luca and sneered. "Americani. Woman!" He threw his hands up in the air in disgust.

"Excuse me?" Opal demanded.

"What is all that shouting for?" Ruby wondered.

"Beats me!" Maude yelled over the noise. They had just entered the lobby and Maude could hardly see two steps in front of her due to the bags Ruby had piled into her arms.

Ruby reached the counter in time to see Opal jumping over the top of the counter with her arms flailing. She was howling what Ruby assumed to be Italian curse words. "Opal, what in the world?"

"You take that back!" Opal shouted.

"Get off! E pazza come una sciocca!" Luca shouted.

Maude dropped the bags and grabbed Opal around the middle. Opal was still flailing around for all her worth. She kept yelling at Bartolo and Luca in a mixture of English and Italian swear words, but the words didn't make sense in either language. Maude carried her outside and held her against the stone wall until Opal calmed down and could be released.

"What in the hell is going on here?" Maude asked.

"He said my mother was a horse and I lived in a pigsty! Well, he said all Americans do and then he said that I was just a woman and all women are stupid. We don't know what we're talking about. I just can't stand for that!" Opal huffed. She paused to take a deep breath and steady herself.

"What was that all about? So embarrassing!" Ruby said as she walked out dragging the bags behind her.

"We oughta let her pummel them again! Those bastards!" Maude yelled.

"Maude! Stop it or they'll hear you!" Ruby hushed her.

"Good! I hope they do! I think it's about time an American woman kicked their asses!" she yelled through the door. "We beat them in the war, we can beat 'em again!"

"Oh my God! Let's get out of here!" Ruby wailed. She tossed bags to Maude and Opal and they hurried down the street. They could hear the two men yelling after them.

"Hurry! Don't look back. Let's get a move on," Ruby said. Once they were comfortably out of sight, Opal asked a passerby for directions and once they were pointed in the right direction, they found the train station easily

As they sat on the train, Opal was still fuming about the two men at the hotel.

"I hope you didn't leave them a tip," Maude told her.

Opal stopped for a moment. "A tip?"

"Don't tell me you left them a tip," Maude stared at her.

"Well, actually, now that you mention it, I don't think we ever got around to paying," Opal admitted.

Ruby was mortified and Maude burst out laughing. "Serves them right for insulting us," Maude said.

"Oh I just don't think that's right," Ruby said.

"Too late now. We're on our way back to Rome," Opal said.

"But won't they try to find us?" Ruby asked.

"What are they going to do? Come to Rhinestone? After insulting us and all of America? I'd like to see them try," Maude said. She rubbed her fist against her other palm and gritted her teeth.

Ruby was still unsure, but she dropped the subject. Opal was right. It was too late to worry about it now. They quickly found themselves laughing at Opal the vigilante and her fight of the century. "You sure slugged that older one," Maude laughed. "Should have let you keep going."

"Well, I guess an international brawl was really the only appropriate way to end this adventure," Ruby laughed.

"And we still have to make it home," Maude said.

"If the good Lord's willing and the creek don't rise, nothing else will happen," Ruby said.

The train pulled into the main station in Rome and they quickly found a cab. They decided to splurge since they had saved a good bit on the hotel, thanks largely to Opal's fight.

Maude was so thankful that this was the last taxi ride in Italy. These people didn't know how to drive like the people in Rhinestone did. She breathed a sigh of relief when they made it safely to the airport.

"It's so crowded! Why is everyone and their mama flying today?" Maude scowled.

Maude and Ruby walked ahead of Opal who was marveling at the rows of flowers. A midnight black kitten meowed softly by the tree. "Ooh, look at you," Opal crooned.

"What was that Opal?" Ruby called over her shoulder.

"Oh, nothing. Just talking to myself," Opal laughed. She leaned down and stuffed the small cat into her oversized bag.

Maude and Ruby shrugged. Opal talking to herself wasn't anything new. They entered the large doors of the airport and heaved their luggage over the steps leading to the check in area.

"Shh, you're fine," Opal whispered.

"Are you ok?" Maude asked. "You're being even weirder than usual."

"Yea, I'm fine," Opal said. "Just excited to get home is all."

"Oddly enough I am, too," Ruby said. "Well, I'm excited to get back to normal. Heck, I don't even know what normal is anymore. Guess nothing's going to be normal now."

"Yea, you're coming back with some exciting news," Maude said.

"Speaking of that," Ruby said. "Let's keep that little secret between us three for now. I'm talking to you in particular Opal." Opal gave her a sheepish smile.

"What are you going to tell your parents? Are you going to tell Jameson? Oooh, his mama ain't going to like this at all," Maude cackled. She was not a fan of Mrs. Montgomery.

"Of course I'll tell Jameson. Eventually. I guess Mrs. Montgomery will either get over it or not. I'm going to tell Jameson that I'm not expecting anything from him. I can do this on my own. I mean, with y'all and my parents, of course. If he doesn't take it well, I mean, not much to be done about it now," Ruby said.

"Jameson's not going to leave you hanging. Reckon what your parents are going to say though?" Opal asked.

"I'm sure they'll take it about as well as y'all two did," Ruby chuckled. "At least I've got the next few hours to think about it."

Ruby and Maude walked up to the check in counter, but were surprised when Opal was missing. They turned around and found her rifling through her suitcase to pull out the cat bag she bought in Turkey from underneath a mound of dirty laundry.

"What are you doing?" Maude asked.

"I just gotta get something real quick," Opal replied.

"What in the world?" Ruby asked walking over to where Opal kneeled beside her bags.

"I just haven't used it yet and it's too pretty to let it sit there. It should enjoy the flight home too," Opal said.

"Of course it should," Maude mumbled.

"Maybe I should get mine out, too," Ruby said.

"For the love of God, will y'all two hurry up!" Maude grumbled.

Once Ruby and Opal had retrieved their bags, they checked in their lugagge and found their gate.

They boarded their flight and found seats across the aisle from each other. Opal shoved her bag underneath her chair and tucked her pillow around it. "That should keep you safe," she whispered.

Maude settled into the seat next to her and started her repetitive deep breaths. "I hate flying," she whispered.

"Yea, that came across loud and clear on the flight over here," Opal laughed.

"Which one?" Maude growled.

"Y'all behave!" Ruby whispered from across the aisle. "We've got two hours till Frankfurt and I think we all need to catch up on some sleep." Ruby pulled her sweater over her arms and closed her eyes.

Opal motioned for the stewardess to come over. "Do you have a tranquilizer gun?" she asked sweetly.

The stewardess looked at her with suspicion. Then she looked over at Maude who was rocking back and forth. She nodded and immediately left. She returned a few moments later with three small bottles of scotch. Opal gave her money and gave two of the bottles to Maude. She kept the third bottle in her pocket in case of emergencies.

"Oh God, here we go," Maude cried. She gripped the armrest tightly and closed her eyes. Opal could hear her mumbling something underneath her breath. Thankfully she was loud enough where no one would ever hear her new friend underneath the seat.

"You okay over there, Maude?" Ruby asked.

"She's going to be fine. I'll take good care of everything. You go ahead and take your nap," Opal told her. She gave a soft kick at the bag underneath her seat and smiled at the attendant who walked by. "We'll be there soon enough," she said to no one in particular.

❦ Chapter Twenty-Five ❦

The flight to Frankfurt passed uneventfully. Opal scampered off the flight quickly leaving Ruby to attend to a sluggish Maude.

"Thanks for your help," Ruby said once they found Opal. "I had to pry her out of the seat."

"I'm fine," Maude slurred. "Where to now?"

"We've got to catch our flight to New York. Hurry up!" Opal said. She wiped her hands on her pants and scurried off.

"What's up with her?" Maude asked.

"It's Opal. Who knows?" Ruby answered. They finally caught up with her in line to board the plane. "Hey, what are you doing?" Ruby asked.

"Huh? Oh, nothing. I um, accidently dropped some of my sandwich into my bag and was just cleaning it out. Yea, I had to clean it out," Opal answered.

Maude looked over at Opal's bag. She really needed to lay off the alcohol on this flight because Opal's bag seemed to be moving of its own accord.

"Ok Maude, in you go," Ruby said. She guided Maude to the first available seat and buckled her in. You stay there and thanks to Opal, here's another little bottle for you.

Opal slid into the row of seats behind Maude next to the window. Ruby settled in next to Opal and thought she caught a glimpse of Opal petting her bag. "You ok Opal?"

"I'm fine," she smiled. She shoved the bag underneath her seat and leaned down to tuck the pillow around it carefully.

"Is there something breakable in there?" Ruby asked.

"You could say that," Opal replied.

"Aw, what did you buy?" Ruby asked.

"Well, I didn't actually buy it. Practically giving it away, you could say," Opal explained. She saw the look of concern flash across Ruby's face. "It's um, it's a surprise."

"I don't want to know," Ruby shook her head and grabbed a magazine from the seat pocket. The less she knew about Opal's grand surprise, the easier the nine hour flight would be.

Maude slept the entire nine hours and woke quite refreshed as the plane landed. She helped Ruby gather her bag and pillow because as soon as the plane landed, Opal leapt over Ruby and said she needed to use the bathroom. She would meet them in a few minutes.

"Something's gotten into her!" Ruby said.

"Something worse than usual?" Maude asked.

"She said she has a surprise for us later," Ruby explained.

"Oh my," Maude chuckled.

"Exactly," Ruby agreed.

Ruby and Maude found a bench near the bathroom exit and waited for Opal. Opal emerged from the bathroom a few minutes later with a wad of paper towels.

"We might as well go too since we're here," Ruby told Maude.

"You watch the bags, Opal," Maude said.

"Will do," Opal replied without looking at them. She was concentrating on her own bag. When Ruby and Maude came out and grabbed their bags from the bench, Opal was nowhere in sight.

"Where in the world did she go off to now?" Maude scowled.

"There she is," said Ruby. She pointed across the way at Opal who was standing in the corner whispering to herself.

"She's lost it," Ruby whispered.

"Opal! Hey Opal? You alright?" Maude called.

Opal looked up with a start and hurried over to where Maude and Ruby were standing. "Y'all ready?"

"Just waiting on you," Maude said curiously. "Need any help with that?"

"No, no, I'm fine. Let's go," Opal said.

They headed to the international baggage claim to gather their luggage and head to customs. The line was much shorter than they expected, probably to the time of night that they arrived.

"I am not looking forward to going through customs with all of these bags," Ruby said.

"Well, if you hadn't bought out the entire souvenir line in every country we've been to," Maude hissed. She was struggling to pull Ruby's two new Italian leather suitcases while pushing her own.

"Opal, could you help me with this bag?" Ruby asked.

"Yea, sure," Opal said nonchalantly. She grabbed the bag from Ruby and hoisted it over her shoulder. "You go first, Ruby. You have the least amount of stuff."

"This ain't all my junk," Maude said bitterly. Opal gave her a gentle shove and then stood in line behind Maude before chatting with the woman behind her.

"We just got back from Italy. Where are you coming from?" Opal asked politely.

"I'm coming from a dig in Greece. I'm an archeologist. It was very exciting," the woman replied.

"Oh, I love Greece. We should have gone there, too, but we ran out of time sightseeing. We did see some rocks and ruins though! Have you ever heard of Pompeii?" Opal asked the woman.

"Yes, of course," the lady said.

"Yeah, we got a few things from there. Those rocks are really something. I hope the folks back home like them. Got a statue from the Pope, too," Opal said.

"You can't bring things from a live dig. You can't bring a lot of things like that back. You'll get in trouble if they catch you," the woman whispered.

"Really, like what?" Opal asked.

"Like historical artifacts, weapons, live animals. There's a whole list," she said.

Opal paused for a moment. "Oh. Well ain't that something," she said tensely. Opal watched as Ruby went through the usual question and answer portion. Maude was next. She passed through her suitcase and began to load Ruby's two leather suitcases onto the roller.

"Maude!" Opal hissed.

"Huh?" she asked.

"That lady behind me said there's a whole list of stuff we can't bring back from Italy!" Opal whispered.

"Like what?" Maude asked.

"She said weapons or rocks or animals," Opal mouthed.

"Why are you whispering? We don't have any of that in our bags. Wait a minute! You've got to be kidding me!" Maude shrieked. "Opal! What the hell did you pack?"

Maude was suddenly surrounded by uniformed men who grabbed the suitcases and began wrenching them open. In the scuffle, Opal slid around the posts and joined Ruby on the other side.

"Where's Maude?" Ruby asked.

"Um, not really sure," Opal smiled. She patted her bag and handed Ruby her own bag. "Hold this for a minute. I need to use the bathroom again."

"Sure you're ok? You've been running back and forth to the bathroom a lot," Ruby said.

"I don't think that sandwich from earlier is sitting well with me," Opal acknowledged. "I'll be back in a few."

Ruby sat back down on a nearby bench and waited for Opal to return. A few minutes later, Maude came through the barrier completely red in the face. "Where is she?" she bellowed.

"Maude? What is going on?" Ruby asked. She jumped to her feet and helped Maude as she struggled with the suitcases.

"I will end her," Maude spit. "Where is she?"

"Maude! Shh! What are you talking about?" Ruby asked again.

"Opal," Maude breathed. "She's done it this time."

"Sit down here," Ruby instructed. "Start from the beginning. What is going on?"

Maude sat down and took a few deep breaths. Before she could tell Ruby what happened, Opal emerged from the bathroom. When she made eye contact with Maude, Maude erupted.

"OPAL!" she roared. "GET OVER HERE!"

Opal dipped back into the bathroom and Ruby stood in front of Maude to keep her from running after Opal. "What in the world?" Ruby shouted.

"She packed rocks in her suitcase! Rocks! Actual rocks, Ruby. They just converged on me!

Grabbed the bags and rifled through them!" Maude shouted.

"Slow down, Maude," Ruby said. "What was in your bag?

"Not mine! Opal's!" Maude yelled. "Opal said something about weapons and rocks and a live animal wasn't allowed and all of a sudden, bam! They're asking questions and holding up a bag full of rocks and a sword wrapped in paper. A sword, Ruby! I barely got through alive."

"Sit here and just breathe. I'll go check on Opal. I think she's really sick. She can hardly stay out of the bathroom," Ruby said.

"Oh God, if she's pregnant, too, then I'm jumping out of the next plane!" Maude huffed.

Ruby rolled her eyes and made her way to the bathroom. She turned around quickly to make sure Maude wasn't following her. To her credit, Maude was sitting cross legged on the bench with her arms folded across her chest. She still looked murderous with rage, but at least she was staying put.

"Opal?" Ruby called gently. "Opal, are you in there?"

"Yes," Opal said timidly.

"Maude's pretty upset, Opal. I think you need to come out here and explain to us what's going on," Ruby said.

Opal came out of the stall and walked past Ruby to wash her hands. "Ok, where's Maude?" Opal asked.

"Right out front. She's all in a tizzy saying security was called and you disappeared. I'm a little confused," Ruby explained. Opal looked confused, too, and followed Ruby back to the bench.

"I'm going to murder you right here!" Maude yelled when she saw Opal behind Ruby.

"Maude! Stop, you're making a scene!" Ruby shushed her.

"Me? I've already been the victim of a scene," Maude yelled back. "You nearly got me arrested!"

"Did you save my sword?" Opal asked. "What about my rocks from Pompeii?"

Maude glared at her and bared her teeth. "Are you kidding me? No I didn't save your sword? Where the hell did you get a sword from?"

"I saw it in a gift shop! The man said it was the tiger killer! And you let them throw away my rocks! I collected those myself!" Opal moaned. "What about the Pope statue? I told my new friend we met him."

"What were you saying about the Pope?" Ruby asked.

"I was just telling my new friend about how we met the Pope in Rome," Opal explained.

"He wasn't the Pope!" Maude and Ruby both said.

"He said he was the Pope," Opal shrugged. "Must have gotten lost in translation. Anyway, can we lose this luggage and get something to eat because I'm starving."

"I thought your stomach was hurting?'" Ruby mentioned.

"All better now. I found some aspirin and allergy medication. I'm good to go," Opal smiled.

"What does aspirin and allergy medicine have to do with an upset stomach?" Maude asked.

"I don't know," Opal admitted. "Seems to have done the trick though!"

"It's Opal. We both know she's wired differently," Ruby said.

"Since you're irritated, why don't you pick what we eat? After we drop off these bags," Opal said.

They made their way to the check-in area, got the boarding passes for the flight back to Atlanta, and dropped off their bags. There was an all night breakfast restaurant near their gate. Maude was thankful they had pancakes and bacon.

"I've missed bacon," Maude said with a smile.

"Maude, we've been gone two weeks. It's not like you were banished for years," Ruby laughed.

Opal was quieter than usual. Ruby assumed she was still feeling poorly. Or maybe she was just tired from their trip. Ruby knew she was certainly exhausted. When Opal ordered two scrambled eggs, Ruby put her hand on her shoulder and asked if she was ok. Opal nodded and when Ruby and Maude weren't looking, she dumped the rest of the scrambled eggs into her bag.

They ate their meal quietly and made their way to the gate to wait for their flight out of New York. Luckily, they were catching the earliest flight of the morning and the waiting area was sparsely populated with sleepy passengers. When the gate was opened for boarding, they joined the queue and ambled onto the plane without the excitement and fanfare of their previous flights along the journey.

Once again, Ruby was sitting beside Opal. Maude sat down in the seat across the aisle from them and quickly fastened her seatbelt. She still didn't like air travel, but she was so exhausted from her ordeal at customs that she might actually be able to sleep without any assistance.

Ruby noticed Opal rifling quickly through her bag. "Ouch!" Opal yelped.

"What?" Ruby asked.

"Paper cut," Opal lied.

"That doesn't look like a paper cut," Ruby said.

"It's nothing, just a little scratch," Opal replied.

"How did you scratch yourself?" Ruby asked

"Something in my bag. It's fine," Opal said quickly.

"What in the world is in there Opal?" Ruby asked. She went to grab the bag from Opal, but Opal snatched it back. It hit the window and something hissed from inside it.

"Oh my God! Is that a snake?" Ruby yelled.

"Keep your voice down! Geez! It's not a snake, Ruby," Opal said.

"Then what was that?" Ruby whispered.

"Can you keep a secret?" Opal asked her.

Ruby glared at her. "Like you can?" she asked.

"Ok, ok. See, what had happened was, I saw this little guy outside the airport and he was so scrawny and lonely. He needed someone to take care of him. Well, he practically jumped in my bag," Opal explained.

"What exactly is it?" Ruby asked through gritted teeth.

"Now, he's just a baby," Opal explained.

"You kidnapped a baby?" Ruby squealed.

It was Opal's turn to glare at Ruby. "It's a baby kitten," Opal whispered.

Ruby shook her head. "You've got to be kidding me! Opal! Is this why you ran away at customs?"

"That was a misunderstanding," Opal reminded her.

"Somehow I don't think Maude thinks it was a misunderstanding!" Ruby said.

"That's because she hasn't met Leonardo yet!" Opal exclaimed.

"Leonardo?" Ruby asked. "Leonardo?"

"What are y'all talking about over there?" Maude asked.

"Nothing," Ruby shook her head. "He is a pretty little kitty, aren't you?" Ruby cooed.

"He doesn't understand a single word you're saying, Ruby," Opal sighed. "He's an Italian cat."

"What different does that make?" Ruby sassed.

"He only speaks Italian!" said Opal. She was a little surprised that it was taking Ruby this long to catch on. "I can't wait to introduce him to Mable when we get home. She will love another little kitty friend."

"Who's Italian? What is going on over here?" Maude was suddenly standing beside Ruby. She stared down at the black kitten sticking its tiny head out of Opal's bag. It looked as though it had been given a little too much to drink during its adventure to the states. "Opal, you didn't," Maude muttered.

"Is that why you've been randomly dumping food into your bag?" Ruby asked

"He was hungry," Opal shrugged.

"Where did you get him from? Don't tell me you stole him!" Maude shook her head. Nothing that Opal did surprised her anymore. "Is that why you made a scene at customs? You stole that lady's cat, didn't you?"

"I didn't steal him!" Opal retorted. "I found him when we were walking into the airport back in Rome. I couldn't leave him all alone!"

"You've had him since Rome?" Maude gasped. "He could've had a family. There's probably more just like him wandering around out there."

"You're right! Should we go back?" Opal asked.

"Oh dear God in heaven," Maude said, sitting back down in her seat and refusing to be party to their conversation any longer. Maude couldn't wait to be out in the fresh air once they landed in Atlanta.

Chapter Twenty-Six

"Shotgun!" Ruby called as they headed toward Maude's car.

"I'll drive!" Opal volunteered.

"Oh no you don't!" Maude yelled behind her.

"What? Why not?" Opal asked innocently.

"You're sitting in the back with the stowaway," Ruby told her.

"You can't put little Leo in the back," Opal said. "He'll get carsick."

"Watch me!" Maude said. She shoved Opal into the backseat and loaded the suitcases and duffel bags around her like a tightly packed igloo. Ruby handed Opal her cat bag and the pillows before pushing the seat back into place. Opal spent the two hours back to Rhinestone wedged in between all the suitcases and bags with her new kitten on her lap. The drugs were wearing off because Leonardo suddenly came alive.

"What's all that noise back there?" Maude asked.

"Look who woke up," Opal cooed. "Did you enjoy your nap, my little Leo?"

"Are you taking pictures of your cat?" Ruby asked.

"He's just so cute!" Opal crooned. She stuck the camera back in his face and Leo hissed loudly before trying to jump through the window. He missed his mark and landed, claws first, on top of Maude's head.

"What the hell?" Maude yelled as she tried to swat the animal away. She flailed her arms over her head. Ruby grabbed the steering wheel and managed to keep them out of the ditch while Maude grabbed the cat and yanked with all her might.

"Opal! Put the camera down and help!" Ruby wailed.

Opal reached up and pulled Leo, but he had decided to hang on for dear life. When she finally jerked the cat off Maude's scalp, he bit her on her finger. She dropped him directly on the back of the driver's seat. He hung on for dear life, but eventually gravity and Maude's driving got the better of him. He slid down the entire length of the seat, leaving perfect claw marks in his wake.

"What was that sound?" Maude asked sternly.

"Oh nothing," Opal said sweetly.

Ruby looked over at Opal and saw the ripped seat. "Can you drop me off first?" she asked quickly.

"I'm going to kill her and that damn cat," Maude mumbled to Ruby.

Ruby smiled but didn't mention anything about the condition of the car seat. That would be a surprise for another time.

"Tell your Mom'n'em that we'll be over Sunday after church for a visit," Maude told her as Ruby closed the car door. "Me, too! I'll bring Leonardo!" Opal called from the backseat.

"I will. As long as y'all don't kill each other before then," Ruby smiled.

"I can't guarantee anything," Maude answered seriously.

Ruby dropped her bags by the front door and went into the kitchen to see her mom and dad.

"I didn't think you were getting home until later," her dad said. He stood up to give her a big hug.

"Maude was driving," Ruby smiled.

"That explains it," he laughed and sat back down to his lunch. "Did you bring me anything?" he teased.

"Well, Opal brought home a cat. I think you'll have to settle for the shirt and some other little trinkets I found," she laughed.

"A cat?" he asked. "Nope, I don't want to know. Ok, yes I do, but give me those bags first."

She handed her dad the bags from her arms and he walked to the porch to collect the rest of her things.

"Oh and thanks for all the letters and postcards you sent home," her mother], Barbara, said from the kitchen sink. She winked at Ruby.

Ruby went over and gave her a big hug. "Sorry about that. We were so busy with everything."

"Did you have a good time, sweetie?" her mother asked.

"It was an adventure I'll never forget," Ruby smiled.

Her dad stumbled back through the front door with her three suitcases. "Looks like you brought home half the world with you. Are these new?" he asked.

"Well, I needed some more room and they were so cute! Do you like them?" Ruby asked.

"Sure, sure," he replied. "God what are in them? They're heavier than a stack of bricks!"

Ruby pointed to the vase of fresh flowers on the table. "Those are pretty!"

"They're from Jameson," her mother smiled.

"I hope you at least sent that boy something. He's been worrying us to death since you left," her dad said.

"Jameson?" Ruby sounded shocked.

"Who else? He's been over here every night waiting to see if you were home yet or not. He's been a real pistol ball, I'll tell you that," her dad said.

"He has?" Ruby gulped. "I, I guess I do need to talk to him."

"You sure do," her dad said. "Boy howdy. You gotta do something about him. He looks sorrier than an old hound dog. I started to run him off on account of how he hurt you, sugar, but your mama wouldn't let me. I think he's learned his lesson though. You need to call him before he shows back up here tonight"

"Oh, I will," Ruby mumbled.

Her mother turned away from the sink and stared at her. "What's the matter?"

"Nothing," Ruby whispered.

"Ruby, what's the matter?" her mother asked again.

"Well," Ruby started. "Mama, Daddy, I need to talk to y'all about something. I um, wasn't feeling so well and Maude made me go to the doctor in Italy."

"Food poisoning or something? Ruby, if you were sick you should have called us!" her dad interrupted.

"Daddy, I don't think this was something I could call home about," Ruby whispered. She bit her bottom lip and started to cry.

"Oh Ruby," her mother said. She rushed over to her daughter and hugged her tightly. "It's going to be alright."

"What?" her dad asked. "Was it something I said?"

"I'm sorry, Mama," Ruby said with a tear in her eye.

Her mother wiped the tear away. "Don't you worry, sweetie. We'll get through this."

"Get through what?" her dad asked. He was very confused.

"It's just, well, Jameson and I," Ruby started to cry.

"Did he hurt you, Ruby?" her dad jumped up. "I'll ring his neck!"

"No Daddy. He doesn't know yet," Ruby said. "I only found out a few days ago for sure."

"He doesn't know what?" her dad said.

"There's worse things in this world than a little one. Right John?" her mother asked.

"A little what?" he asked.

Ruby's mother hugged her tightly and said, "Ruby's gonna be a mama."

Her father sat there and said nothing. For a long moment he merely stared off into space.

"Now John," her mother started.

"Daddy, please don't be mad," Ruby said.

"Now I'm not mad at you, sugar, but I'm gonna kill that boy," he answered stoically.

"Daddy no!" Ruby yelped.

"Shh, your daddy's only kidding, Ruby," her mother said sternly. "Right John?"

"I think I need to go out back and chop some firewood," John said. He stood up and kissed Ruby on the top of her head and then marched out the back screen door.

"He'll be alright. He just needs to cool down a little bit," her mother said.

"But should he cool down with an axe in his hands?" Ruby asked.

"Well, just as long as Jameson doesn't show up anytime soon, it'll be fine," her mother said with a slight grimace.

Ruby and her mother spent the afternoon unpacking and talking. By the time that Jameson rang the doorbell that evening, Ruby's mother answered the door and told him that Ruby would meet him on the front porch in a few minutes.

When Ruby stepped onto the porch a few minutes later, Jameson was swinging in the porch swing absentmindedly kicking his feet back and forth.

"Hey Ruby!" he said. His voice squeaked out of excitement, but he tried to cover it with a cough. He stood up and went to hug her, but settled for an awkward handshake at the last minute.

"Hi Jameson," she said softly. She sat in the rocking chair opposite him. He was hoping she would sit beside him on the swing, but he settled for what he could get.

"Your daddy doesn't look too happy to see me," Jameson winced. Mr. Lawrence was looking out the window watching them closely.

"Oh, you have no idea," Ruby mumbled.

"Yea, I think I wore out my welcome the day after you left. I just wanted to know if they'd heard from you is all," he smiled. "So, how's your summer been so far?" he asked sheepishly.

"Adventurous," she replied. "That's for sure," she added under her breath.

"The Stone Sisters take on Italy! What was your favorite thing that you did or saw?" he asked.

Ruby bit her lip and thought hard. "Well, between getting stuck in a monsoon in Nepal, crash landing in Albania, and Opal pushing Maude off a cliff in Positano, Italy, it's really hard to say," Ruby laughed.

"Wait a minute. Did you say Nepal? Albania?" Jameson asked.

Ruby nodded. "I gained quite a few stamps on my passport. We took a few detours before we finally made it to Italy. Long, really long, story," she added.

"Let me guess. Opal?" he laughed.

"How'd you guess?" she smiled.

"But y'all went cliff diving in Positano? Wow!" Jameson said. "That's amazing. I've got to admit that I'm kind of surprised you and Maude went along with that, but that doesn't surprise me about Opal in the least."

"Well, Maude didn't exactly want to jump, but Opal pushed her and well, that's a whole other story," Ruby chuckled again.

"Did Opal push you, too?" he asked.

"No, I didn't um, make that hike up the cliff," she mumbled.

"Oh, ok. Well, I can't wait to hear all about it. If you'd like to sit down and tell me about it. I've got all the time in the world for you, Ruby," Jameson stuttered. He could tell Ruby was being guarded. He didn't blame her one bit. She probably already had another boyfriend in some fancy country halfway across the world.

"Oh and we met the Pope," Ruby added absentmindedly.

"You met the Pope?" he asked.

"Not really, but Opal swears he was the Pope," Ruby clarified.

"Oh, right," he stammered.

They fell into an uneasy silence both having so much to say but neither knowing exactly how to say it.

"Ruby?" he asked timidly.

"Yea?"

"I've got to admit, I've really been missing you. These past few weeks have been torture without you. I know I said I needed time to think about things and I needed to get ahead of my studies, but I was stupid. I'm so sorry Ruby. I know saying I'm sorry won't ever be enough and you probably met a thousand different guys over there on your trip, but I'm really hoping you'll give me another chance. I'll do anything! Ruby, I've got a ring and everything. I'll do anything to win you back!" Jameson started to cry. He was down on one knee.

It broke Ruby's heart to see him in pain. "Say something Ruby," he whimpered.

"Jameson, so much has happened," Ruby began.

"But there's nothing that's happened that can't be undone. We belong with each other. I can't think without you here," he said.

"Well, actually," Ruby stammered.

"There's nothing that will make me stop loving you, Ruby," Jameson said.

She looked at him.

"Marry me?" he asked.

"What?" Ruby asked.

He was down on his knees and pulled a ring from his pocket. "I mean it, Ruby. I'm lost without you. I don't want to lose you. I realized that when you were gone. I can't think. I can't eat. Nothing makes sense. I can't work or study or sleep!"

Ruby sat there in shock.

"I haven't asked your daddy yet, but I think he knows it's coming. I know this isn't really traditional, but please say yes, Ruby. Please say that I haven't messed up for good," he said.

Ruby still couldn't speak.

"I'm ready right now to settle down and start a family," he added quickly. "Anything you want. You name it and I'll do it."

"But what about your parents?" Ruby asked.

"I told them I loved you and I want to marry you!" he said. He stood up and hugged her tightly.

"I'm sure she took that well," Ruby whispered.

"I told them if they didn't like it, they could either get over it or under it because I'm not changing my mind. They know I'm serious. But Ruby, I don't care if anyone approves or not. If you'll have me, that's the only approval I'll ever need."

Ruby suddenly regained her composure.

"Jameson, I've got something I need to say," Ruby said

.

Acknowledgments

This book is only possible because two friends worked together and made it so. We would never have been able to finish this book so quickly without the love and support of our families and friends. To our children and grandchildren, once again we hope we haven't embarrassed you too much with this next installment of the Magnolia Manor series.

For our spouses and partners in crime, thank you for doing the dishes and taking out the trash so we didn't have to nag y'all while we wrote. One of these days maybe y'all will be featured in this tale.

To all of our family members who have inexplicably been mentioned in these pages, whether by name or not, we thank you for supplying is with laughter and stories for at least one more book.

Finally we'd like to thank the ladies at Southern Willow Publishing. Jaimie, Jennifer, and Victoria continue to believe in us and support our many wacky ideas. It is due to their professionalism and experiences that we have been able to publish not one, but two, books already this year. We look forward to many more adventures ahead.

About the Authors

Wanda Jennings and Louise Turner have known each other since the sandbox. They began their writing careers later in life after retiring from their professional careers in civil service and social work.

When not writing the Magnolia Manor series, Louise and Wanda enjoy traveling, spending time with their families, and learning how to quilt.

Dear Reader,

We hope you enjoyed *Saints & Sinners*. We are truly blessed that you took the time (again) to spend a few hours with some of our favorite members of the Rhinestone gang. Rhinestone has a collection of true characters, that's for sure! It's hard to not fall in love with them.

We are currently working on the next book in the Magnolia Manor series. This next book will be all about discovering what all the Stone Sisters and their families have been up to during the sixty year gap between the first two novels. If you enjoyed *Dirty Laundry* and *Saints & Sinners*, please make sure to join us on our next adventure in *Color Me Crazy!*

Thank you again for reading *Saints & Sinners*. We would really appreciate it if you could take a few minutes and leave us a positive review on Amazon.com and Goodreads.com. Your feedback is very important to us and it helps spread the word about our series.

Thank you again for humoring two old ladies. We always wanted to share the Rhinestone gang with the world and we are so thankful that we found a way to do it. We look forward to a long line of books in this series

Love,
Louise & Wanda

The adventures will continue this winter. Join Opal, Maude, Ruby, and the whole Rhinestone gang in

Color Me Crazy!

Available Winter 2020!